Beetles,
Lightly Toasted

~~~~~~~~~~~~~~~

PHYLLIS REYNOLDS NAYLOR

~~~~~~~~~~~~~~~

A Yearling Book

Published by
Bantam Doubleday Dell Books for Young Readers
a division of
Bantam Doubleday Dell Publishing Group, Inc.
1540 Broadway
New York, New York 10036

ISBN: 0-440-40143-7

Reprinted by arrangement with Macmillan Publishing Co., Inc.

Printed in the United States of America

March 1989

20   19   18   17   16   15   14

OPM

For J. P. and his friends

Contents

Beetles,
Lightly Toasted

1

Remembering Roger

A SQUARE OF LIGHT FROM THE KITCHEN WINDOW shone on the wet grass as Andy followed his father to the barn, pulling on Big Earl's jacket as he went. At five-thirty in the morning the shapes of the barn, the silo, the grain bin, and the hog house were barely visible in the mist.

He and his father never did much talking while the cows were milked. Later, when the two went back to the kitchen for sausage and eggs, things would get lively, but out here in the early morning the farm had the look of strange objects in a strange land. Andy pretended that the wooden plank, stretched across the mud in the barnyard, was a narrow footbridge leading to a cave, and when he swung back the heavy barn door, he suddenly saw, from out of the shadows . . . !

The story usually ended there, because the first thing Big Earl did when he reached the barn was turn on the lights, and the second thing was turn on the radio—station WMT from Cedar Rapids—with the news, the farm prices, and a little country music in between.

"Soothes the bossies," Andy's father always said.

The barn gave off a rich hay and animal smell, and as Andy and his father approached the stalls, the cows turned their heads, their huge eyes searching out the farmer. Some mooed and shifted impatiently. Sometimes Andy pretended that the black-and-white holsteins were twenty hunchbacked prisoners who had been kept in a cave all their lives on bread and water, and all Andy had to do to set them free was give them each a shovelful of energy-building grain before the guards came rushing in.

While Big Earl cleaned the cows' udders with a brush and soap and attached the soft rubber cups of the milking machine, Andy quickly spread a shovelful of grain in front of each stall.

"One for you, and one for you . . ." he murmured under his breath, hurrying.

But the guards, the seven yellow cats and one gray tom, were already rousing themselves from where they'd slept on rafters and feed sacks, and were jumping down to the floor, swarming down the hay mow right toward him.

Shovel, shovel, shovel . . . Andy leaped over the gray tom in time to feed the thirteenth cow, but then one of the yellow cats came up from behind and rubbed against his legs, and he'd been caught. The object was to see if he could feed all twenty prisoners before he was touched by a guard.

The holsteins munched noisily while the machine did the milking and an old Glen Campbell song played on. A short time later, Earl poured the white liquid into a stainless-steel receptacle, leaving a little warm milk behind in a pan for the cats. It steamed in the chilly April air.

"I'll try again tomorrow," Andy whispered to the last cow as he put the feed shovel away and picked up the manure shovel, returning once more to the first stall. He wanted to see how many stalls he could clean before breakfast.

Except for the milking and a few other chores, Andy's father usually didn't work on Sundays. Sundays were reserved for going to church, for eating slowly, and for reading the *Bucksville Gazette*. But it was planting time, and after the rain of the past few weeks, tractors were going all over Iowa. This afternoon, in fact, Uncle Delmar would be over to help plant the fields, and they would work right into the evening by headlights, if necessary.

Andy wished that the day were over just so it could be evening, because as soon as it was evening, it was practically night, and when the night was over it would be tomorrow which was the day he had been waiting for all year—the last *two* years, in fact—the start of the annual Roger B. Sudermann Contest.

If Andy could win this contest, his father would hear the news some morning on station WMT and his mother would read about it in the *Gazette*. The winner would be announced at school, and Andy would be presented with the Roger B. Sudermann Award on the steps of the Bucksville Library.

To tell the truth, nobody could remember exactly who Roger B. Sudermann was. Lois, Andy's sister, had gone to school with him back in fifth grade, but she couldn't remember if he was the kid who was stung on the lip by a bee, or the one who came to school on Halloween dressed as a TV set. It didn't much matter, though, because that was the year that Roger Sudermann fell off the top of a silo and died and his father, Luther Sudermann, publisher of the *Gazette,* set up a special award in memory of his son. It was to be presented annually to the fifth grader of Bucksville Elementary who showed the most inventiveness and imagination in an essay contest, subject to be announced. Tomorrow was the day the subject would be announced, because it was Roger B. Sudermann's birthday, or would have been if he were alive. The winner of the contest would be named on June 4, and the award presented on June 10, which was the day Roger died.

"Creepy, if you ask me," Lois said once. "I wonder if he *was* the one who came to school as a TV set."

The first year of the contest, the subject of the essay was "If You Had a Million Dollars, How Would You

Spend It?" The winner was a girl who said she would divide it between all fifty states so that each of them could start its own Roger B. Sudermann contest. Naturally, everybody thought that maybe the award itself would be a million dollars, since Luther Sudermann had so much money, but all the winner got was a check for fifty dollars and a little bronze pin that said "Imagination" that came unglued a week after she'd worn it. Her picture was in the newspaper, though, and because Luther Sudermann had connections, it was announced on WMT as well.

The next year the subject for the essay contest was, "If You Could Communicate with Animals, What Would You Say?" and the year after that, "Is Spiderman Possible?" That year, the fifth-grade class was supposed to come up with scientific ways to stick to walls.

Andy had been trying to guess what the subject for this year's essay would be. You only had one chance to enter the contest, when you were in the fifth grade at Roger's school. Andy had been writing down possible topics in the back of his old green notebook, ideas such as "Could Human Beings Hibernate?" and "How I Would Catch the Loch Ness Monster." He'd even written out whole paragraphs for some of his ideas so he'd have a head start.

Andy had shoveled out nine of the stalls when he realized that his dad had already let the cows out to pasture. The whole family would be up by now, gathered around for breakfast at the big table, Sunday school lessons perched on the edge along with the cream and butter and piles of toast and bacon. Aunt Wanda would be frying potatoes as fast as she could to keep up with Wayne and Wendell, and Lois would be searching for the comics, while Mother put the finishing touches on a pie for the noon meal.

Andy put his shovel in the corner and went on back to the house. After washing his hands he slid into his seat at the table. Aunt Wanda picked up his plate without asking and put a fried egg on it that left a thin trail of yellow yolk from the skillet all the way across his napkin. Runny eggs, in fact any foods that wiggled, were not on his list of favorites so Andy tried not to look at it as he drank his orange juice.

"Have you got *Gasoline Alley?*" Lois asked Wayne, trading sections of the Sunday comics.

"Save the *Food* section," said Aunt Wanda, piling fried potatoes next to Andy's egg, so that the grease from the potatoes ran into the egg yolk and made Andy's stomach flutter. "Don't want anybody shining their shoes on my recipe pages, now."

Andy ignored his egg and potatoes and filled up on toast instead. He didn't mind Sundays; didn't mind church; didn't mind farm work at all. What he minded was the cousin who would be coming over that afternoon with Uncle Delmar and Aunt Bernadine. If he could put Jack Barth on the next load of hogs going to market, he'd do it. He might even ship Aunt Wanda off, too. But he refused to let them spoil his Sunday—he didn't want anything to get in the way of his excitement about tomorrow.

He wanted to win that contest in the worst way. All the rest of his family had had their names in the newspaper —even Aunt Wanda. Everyone else had won a prize or made a team or invented a recipe, but there weren't all that many things you could do to get your name in the paper when you were ten. Even Jack the Genius hadn't had his name in the paper yet. The only other ten-year-old Andy could remember ever having made the newspaper—besides Roger Sudermann, of course, when he died—was a girl who owned a rooster with two heads. She'd kept it in a cage down at the Exxon station so folks could see it, but then some high-school boys from Wadena had come by one night and stolen it.

Andy didn't care much about that rooster. A two-headed rooster that couldn't help itself wasn't the same as *doing* something that would make the newspaper or get your name announced on WMT. He wanted to be a farmer like his dad, and he didn't mind if he stayed right there on the farm for the rest of his life, because he liked being his own boss and he loved being outdoors. But he didn't want to just disappear in the corn and soybeans forever, like some folks seemed to do. He didn't want, if somebody were asked where Andy Moller's farm was, to have the somebody answer, "Who?" So when he saw a chance to get his name in the paper, he wasn't just going to walk on by.

In twenty-four hours, Mrs. Haynes would stand in front of the fifth-grade classroom with the official letter from Luther Sudermann and make that grand announcement: "Well, class, the topic for this year's contest is . . ." And Andy would begin.

2

<hr>

Veggies

AT SUNDAY DINNER AUNT WANDA PLACED THE STEAM-
ing bowl of tomatoes and okra on the table directly in
front of Andy and sat down on the other side. *Blurp,
blurp,* went little bubbles in the okra, and the surface rose
and fell as though it were breathing. Andy half expected
the slimy green pods to ooze up over the side of the dish
and slither across the table.

Stay! his eyes warned. Food that was slimy was even
worse than food that wiggled.

All heads were bowed but Andy's. He was still ward-
ing off the okra. Jack was sitting right across from him,
beside Aunt Wanda. Aunt Bernadine and Uncle Delmar
were there too. Counting Andy's family—his parents,

Earl and Edna; his older brothers, Wayne and Wendell; and his sister, Lois—that made ten in all.

Andy felt a kick under the table from Jack and quickly bowed his head. He was tempted to kick back, but was afraid he might get Aunt Wanda.

"Come-Lord-Jesus-be-our-guest-and-let-these-gifts-to-us-be-blest," said Big Earl Moller. "Amen."

At the "Amen," all elbows and arms began moving and the Mollers' big kitchen was filled with voices and the steady clink of serving spoons.

The two families often got together for dinner after church on Sundays—Sundays and just about any occasion whatever—because Edna, Wanda, and Bernadine were sisters.

The two farms, the Mollers' and the Barths', were side by side in Bucksville, fifty miles from Waterloo. At planting time, harvest time, and hog-butchering time, the Barths came over to help out on the Mollers' 400 acres; then the Mollers drove over to help out on the Barths' 475. Afterward they all sat down together at either the Barths' or the Mollers' for Bernadine Barth's fried chicken, Edna Moller's cherry pies, and Aunt Wanda's okra, onion, and tomato casserole, for which she was famous throughout Fayette County. Andy couldn't understand how anyone could be famous for okra.

He helped himself to a piece of cornbread and spread it thickly with butter. His father and Uncle Delmar were talking brood sows.

"Each one of 'em gives me about twenty piglets a year," Earl said.

"Wish mine did as good," said Uncle Delmar. "Figure mine give me eighteen apiece, maybe."

Edna, Wanda, and Bernadine were having a three-way conversation about plum preserves, Lois was listening in, and Wayne and Wendell weren't saying anything, just pitching food down like hay into a wagon.

Jack made a face at Andy. "You eat like a pig," he sneered. He always said that Andy made noises when he ate, but Andy never thought so.

"You eat like a worse one," said Andy.

"Got a face that would stop a truck," Jack said.

"You got a face a truck wouldn't even stop for. Just run right over," Andy retorted.

He only does that way for attention, Mother had told Andy once. *If you gave him a bit of time when he came over, he wouldn't be like that.*

Maybe so, Andy thought, but he sure didn't have much luck with cousins. Jack had been a pest as far back as Andy could remember; he had been born to Aunt Bernadine and Uncle Delmar when they were older than most people were who had children, and because of that they seemed to think that Jack was something special. He and Andy were about the same age and were in the same grade at school, but Aunt Bernadine never let anyone forget that whatever Andy could do, Jack could do better.

"Only thing that boy can't do is walk on water,"

Aunt Wanda grumbled once when Aunt Bernie was bragging about Jack again. But of course Aunt Wanda never had a good thing to say about children at all, never having had any herself.

Watching his cousin across the table, Andy thought about all the times when they were younger that Jack, who had been taller, had lured him into the cornfield, then run off laughing and left him, Andy being too short to see over the top of the stalks. It was like being lost in the forest, and it had taken Andy a while to realize that if he just followed one row as far as it would go, he'd eventually get to somewhere. Now he imagined the okra rising up out of the dish like an octopus, slithering across the table, picking up Jack with one long tentacle, and dragging him out the door.

The Barths all looked like vegetables to Andy. Jack, with his long, narrow bleached-out face, looked like a parsnip; Uncle Delmar looked liked a carrot—same long face as Jack's, but more color; Aunt Bernadine, with her round cheeks and lumpy arms, looked like cauliflower.

Too late, he saw Aunt Wanda reaching across the table for his plate.

"Bowl's too hot to send around," she called out. "Just pass your plates to me."

"I don't want any," Andy said, but before the last word was out, she had deposited a big blob of okra, green and gooey, there beside the cornbread. *Touching* the cornbread! Jack laughed out loud.

Aunt Wanda's a pickled beet, Andy said under his breath, and made a little wall around the okra with his mashed potatoes so that the slime couldn't get through to his chicken. The edge of the mashed potatoes was turning green. *Gross.*

Across the table Jack was imitating him, building a wall out of *his* mashed potatoes. When Andy took a bite of something, Jack took a bite. When Andy lifted his glass of milk, Jack lifted his.

Suddenly Andy lifted his right elbow and gave Wendell a sharp jab in the arm.

"Watch it!" said Wendell, and went on eating.

Jack lifted *his* right elbow . . . and found Aunt Wanda looking down at him. This time *Andy* laughed.

He wished the meal were over. That the *afternoon* were over, in fact, the planting done, and that the Barths had gone home. He never enjoyed meals much when they were there. He was always amazed that some people actually liked everything on the table. His brothers, for example, didn't ask what anything was—didn't even turn their food over to see what was underneath—just wolfed it down. Andy loved to eat too, but you couldn't put any old thing in your mouth and expect to swallow it. Anything with a name like brussel sprouts, for example. Anything with gravy. Weird-sounding foods like lima beans. Gray-looking foods like oatmeal.

He could feel the April breeze on the back of his neck from the open window. The pages of the feed-store calendar fluttered on the wall. In the corner Aunt Wanda's grandfather clock, the only thing she'd brought with her when she came to live with the Mollers, chimed one-thirty. Exactly twenty hours from now, Mrs. Haynes would announce the contest.

And then Aunt Wanda said it: "Andy, don't tell me you ate everything but my Okra Surprise!"

Andy smiled weakly and pushed the okra across the plate with his fork, as if maybe he'd get around to it, maybe he wouldn't.

"You sure don't take after your pa," said Uncle Delmar. "Not a thing on the table your pa won't try."

"I had a finicky eater in my family, I wouldn't know what to do with him!" Aunt Bernadine declared. "Why, Jack eats everything on his plate and then some!"

Jack was grinning. "You work him hard enough, he'll eat anything. Get him shoveling out the barn for you, Uncle Earl. That'll do it."

"Andy does his share of shovelin', now, don't you worry," Big Earl said, smiling at Andy.

But the Barths didn't give up.

"When *I* was in fifth grade, I'd eat everything but the tablecloth," said Uncle Delmar. "Husky kid like you shouldn't be scared off by a little okra."

Aunt Wanda nodded, fixing Andy with her little beet-red eyes.

Andy pushed too hard with his fork, and this time the

slimy green pods went right over the edge of his plate and oozed down onto the blue-checked oilcloth.

That night, Andy dreamed that he was making V-8 juice in a giant blender, dropping the vegetables in one at a time: first the parsnips, then the carrots, then the beets and the cauliflower.

3

$$\sim\sim\sim\sim\sim\sim\sim\sim\sim\sim\sim\sim\sim\sim\sim\sim$$

The Announcement

ANDY STOOD AT THE MAILBOX AT THE END OF THE
lane, books tucked inside the zipper of his jacket. He
watched the clouds swirling up over the horizon, like beef
broth boiling on the stove—sort of scummy looking and
gray. A drop of rain hit his cheek; another hit his eyelid.

After the Barths had gone home the evening before,
Andy's father and brothers had gone back out to the west
field and finished sowing the corn. They'd wanted to plant
the soybeans today and plow the south field, because the
radio had predicted only a twenty percent chance of rain.

The whine of the school bus came from far down the
road—a road so straight that sometimes, when Andy
looked out on it from the roof of the barn, it looked like
a thousand yardsticks joined end to end, with not a curve

or ripple anywhere. The bus was stopping just beyond the pine windbreak that signaled Dora Kray's house, and Andy could see a splash of yellow—Dora in her yellow raincoat—getting on. Then the bus moved forward again, and by the time it reached the mailbox marked "Moller," the tires made wet smacking sounds on the black asphalt and the windshield wipers were going full speed. That meant that Wayne and Wendell would probably drive to the high school after all. Andy knew that his father was standing in the kitchen right now, with his ear beside the radio there on the shelf, listening for a forecast and deciding what to do.

"Hi, Andy," said the driver, a large woman in green slacks and a leather jacket.

Thwang! A paper wad hit Andy on the forehead as he started down the aisle, and he looked halfway back to where a blond-haired boy was laughing. Andy slid in beside him and whacked him on the arm, laughing too.

"Happy Roger B. Sudermann's birthday," Russ Zumbach said to him.

"Yeah," Andy grinned. "Today's the day."

"I hope the essay's about astronauts," Russ said.

"Yeah," Andy said again. He had a couple of ideas in his green notebook himself about astronauts and outer space. While Russ talked on, though, Andy was thinking about who he'd be competing against for the contest. Russ Zumbach probably knew more about spelling and punctuation than anyone else in the class, but he was a little short on imagination. Once, Mrs. Haynes had given the class three minutes to write down all the things they could think of to do with a brick. Andy had thought of fourteen. Russ had only thought of two: put it in the wall of a house and hold a door open with it.

The bus was stopping again, this time beside a metal mailbox with a painted cardinal and the name, "Barth." Jack got on, and Andy was glad that Dora Kray was sitting in the seat just behind him, or Jack would have sat there and bugged him all the way to school.

Andy thought about Dora. She was a possible winner, too. She couldn't spell as well as Russ, but she had thought of twelve things to do with a brick, including press flowers with it, which hadn't occurred to Andy at all. Worry tickled him somewhere beneath his jacket.

Still another fifth grader, Sam Hollins, could probably win the contest, except that he didn't want to enter it, and nobody *had* to enter. The big worry, the kind of worry that came to Andy at night and sat on his chest, was that his cousin Jack would win it. Jack could think of *fifty* things to do with a brick, all of them bad.

The bus was turning now onto the state highway and then, a little further on, it turned again and pulled into the drive of the school.

Sam Hollins and his cousin Travers, with skin the color of gravy, were sitting on the wall by the steps when the bus stopped. They were two cousins who got along well. When they passed each other in the halls, they didn't say, "Hi, Snotnose," the way Jack and Andy did. They'd say, "Hey, man, gimme five!" or something, and slap each other's hands.

"Hey, man!" Sam called as Andy got off the bus.

"Hi, Sam," Andy said.

The rain that had started had now stopped, and it looked as though the clouds overhead would roll on by. Andy felt glad for his father. He leaned against the wall where Sam was sitting.

"Guess what I've got in my lunch bucket," Sam said, their usual morning routine.

Almost everything Andy liked seemed to turn up in Sam Hollins' lunch bucket. Sam had given him a piece of his chicken once, and it was all spicy, spices Andy had never tasted in his own kitchen. Sam had given him a biscuit once, too, and it was so buttery it just seemed to slide down Andy's throat. Sam's family had moved to Bucksville about a year ago. His parents owned the Soul Food Kitchen and Carry-Out downtown on North and Main, and every time Sam opened his lunch box at school, it made Andy want to eat there.

"Chicken," Andy guessed.

"What else?"

"Cornbread."

"What else?"

"Cherry pie."

"Right dessert, wrong pie," grinned Travers.

"Apple."

"Cold and getting colder," said Travers.

"Sweet potato pie," Sam told him.

Andy simply could not understand why, with all the marvelous things Sam's parents cooked in the Soul Food Kitchen, they would make a pie out of sweet potatoes. He didn't even like the sound of the words: sweet potatoes. Potatoes weren't supposed to be sweet. They had the same sound as "sour cream." He was glad that the bell rang just then and he didn't have to tell Sam that sweet potato pie was about as far down on the list as Aunt Wanda's Okra Surprise.

As Travers went on up the hall to sixth grade, Andy squeezed through the door ahead of Sam and Russ and hung up his jacket in the fifth-grade coatroom. Jack was chattering away over by the window. Andy dived into his seat. On the blackboard, in yellow chalk, Mrs. Haynes had written, "Today is the start of the Roger B. Sudermann Contest."

As the students milled about, turning in their arithmetic papers and sharpening pencils, Andy wondered if the contest meant as much to anyone else in the room as it did to him. It was partly that he would like, for once in his life, to win something. He had heard of people who'd won millions of dollars in state lotteries. Uncle Delmar had once won a turkey at the supermarket just by dropping his name in a box. Russ Zumbach had won a free lesson on an oboe, and Dora Kray had won a box of colored pencils for selling the most raffle tickets for her church. Andy hadn't won anything. Not a turkey or an oboe lesson or a single colored pencil.

He could use that prize money, too. He'd always wanted a chemistry set, for one thing. Or maybe he could buy his own piglet from Dad and start raising his own brood sow.

But when you came right down to it, the main reason Andy wanted to win that contest was that he would get not only his name in the newspaper, as he'd been dreaming about on Sunday, but his picture as well.

None of the other Mollers had ever had their pictures in the paper, not even Mother when she'd won a prize at the county fair for her quilt with the "churn dasher" pattern. The quilt was in the paper, but Mother wasn't. When Andy's dad bought a hundred acres from old Mr. Brewer, who owned the farm just north of theirs, and when Lois joined the girls' baseball team, they were mentioned in the *Bucksville Gazette* but there wasn't any photograph. Even when Wayne and Wendell had won fourth place at the state fair for their prize porker, and the photographer had taken a picture of the pig, there had only been a piece of Wayne's foot in the background.

But Andy had never seen his name in print and certainly not his picture. He hadn't even made the newspaper the day he was born; the hospital had mistakenly left his name off the list of babies born that week. He just *had* to win this contest; it was only right.

And then he realized that Mrs. Haynes was standing

up in front of the class holding an envelope.

"Well, you all know what today is," she said. "Last year at least fifteen fifth graders entered the contest, and I hope that most of you will want to try it, too. So . . ." She looked around the room, smiling. "Are we ready to find out what this year's essay topic will be?"

"Yes!" everyone yelled.

Mrs. Haynes picked up her letter opener and slit the envelope. "We have certainly had some interesting subjects in the past, haven't we? Talking to animals, Spiderman . . ." She took out a folded sheet of paper and opened it up. As her eyes scanned the sheet, Andy thought he saw a slight frown forming on her forehead.

Read it out loud! he wanted to yell. What was she waiting for?

"Well, class," the teacher said finally, "As you know, it's Mr. Sudermann who chooses the topic, and this year, the subject for the essay will be 'Conservation.' "

All the excitement Andy had felt earlier seemed to dissolve into a puddle of cold water at the bottom of his stomach. A murmur went around the class that didn't have any particular sound to it, certainly not "Oh!" or "Wow!" If there was any word in the murmur at all, it was "Ugh."

4

The Dirty, Rotten Sneak

ANDY FINISHED HIS CHORES AFTER SCHOOL, SCARCELY aware of his hands on the shovel as he cleaned out the stalls.

It's not fair, he thought again and again, chasing a red hen out of the barn, as though her egg laying in the haystack instead of the chicken house were the cause of his problems. One of the most boring words in the English language, as far as Andy was concerned, was "conservation." It was important, all right, especially to farmers, but it wasn't exactly a fun thing to write about. Even Mrs. Haynes had thought so. Andy had known by the look on her face.

She had gone on to read the rest of Mr. Sudermann's letter out loud:

Conservation can be almost anything: improving our soil; making the most of our food supply; saving energy; budgeting money. . . . Put your imaginations to work! Start with something you already have and see how far you can stretch it. Invention's the name of the game.

That didn't help. Every time Andy thought of all the topics that Mr. Sudermann *could* have chosen, he got angry all over again.

"Let's boycott the contest," he said at recess as a group of disgruntled fifth graders gathered by the fence. "If nobody enters, Mr. Sudermann will have to come up with something better."

"A boycott!" Russ said. "That's it! Let's tell the others. If a whole week goes by and nobody signs up for the contest, Mrs. Haynes will have to call Mr. Sudermann and tell him the topic stinks."

"I'll bet all those other essay topics were just to get people interested in the contest. Now it just sounds like school," Dora Kray added. Dora was as freckled as a sparrow's egg, and when she was angry, the freckles seemed to grow darker. "Who wants to write about soil and water?"

Not Andy, that's for sure. A boycott was just what they needed! He put the shovel back in the corner and had just started for the field when he saw Dad and Wayne and

Wendell bringing in the tractor. They must have finished planting the soybeans, because they had the same look on their faces that Mom and Aunt Wanda had after they'd finished canning—when the tomatoes and beans and rhubarb and beets were all packed away in jars, row upon row of them, in the cellar. Even okra looked vaguely appetizing when it was in a jar and not sliding around on someone's plate.

With a grinding roar, the tractor came crawling between the hog house and the tool shed, Wayne hanging onto the back.

"You get the soybeans planted?" Andy yelled up at his father.

Earl Moller grinned and nodded.

"You plow the south field?"

"Yep!" Earl sang out. Wayne jumped down and followed Wendell into the hog house, but Andy's dad motioned him over to the tractor: "Mother wants her vegetable garden plowed," he shouted. "How about it?"

Andy didn't have to be asked twice. He was good with machines, and sometimes, when there wasn't any hurry, his father let him drive the tractor himself.

Big Earl got down as Andy took his place. His heart thumping excitedly, Andy could feel the power beneath him as he moved the tractor forward. Carefully, he steered it down the lane and into the half-acre lot between the house and the road where Mother and Aunt Wanda grew their vegetables. Who cared about a dumb old contest, anyway? This was what Andy liked to do more than anything else in the world.

When he got just the angle he wanted, he lowered the four-bottom plow and moved slowly along the edge of the garden, turning occasionally to watch the black earth churning up behind him, smelling the wonderful scent of spring soil. Usually it was Dad or Wayne or Wendell who plowed the garden, and it was Andy who ran barefoot in the dirt behind, feeling the rich dark earth squish up between his toes. But this time it was Andy up in the driver's seat, Andy doing the job. Who cared about getting your name in the newspaper, having it announced in a school assembly, and receiving the Roger B. Sudermann Award on the steps of the Bucksville Library?

Andy did.

On Tuesday, the sheet of paper tacked to the bulletin board in Mrs. Haynes' classroom remained blank. Nobody had signed up for the contest. Not a single person.

So far, so good, Andy thought.

On Wednesday, as Mother was packing Andy's lunch for school, she asked, "Weren't you supposed to find out about that essay contest this month?"

Andy took the sandwich she gave him, thickly filled with ham and lettuce, and put it in the center of his lunch bucket, squeezed between a slice of Aunt Wanda's chocolate cake and an orange.

"I already heard," he said.

Lois looked up from the table where she was eating toast and reading the comics. "What's the topic? Something weird?"

Andy's lips barely moved: "Conservation."

"Conservation! *Yawn!*" Lois said.

"Are we talking about the same contest?" asked Mother.

"Yes, but we're all going to boycott it. Everyone else is mad about it too."

"Well, I don't know, now. Think about it, Andy." Mother said.

"I have," Andy told her. "And it stinks."

By Friday, the sign-up sheet on the bulletin board was still blank. Russ said he certainly hadn't thought of anything to write, and at recess, Dora took a poll and said that everyone she'd talked to was still in favor of the boycott. Andy smiled to himself. Mrs. Haynes had begun to look worried.

"Think about it, class," she said, sounding just like Andy's mother.

"Let Mr. Sudermann think about it," Andy muttered under his breath. He had other things on his mind at the moment. He may not ever have won a free oboe lesson or a box of colored pencils, but Lois had asked if he wanted to be batboy this year for her baseball team, the *Bucksville Beagles,* and get a free T-shirt.

"Sure!" Andy had said. Might as well. He and Mom and Aunt Wanda usually went to all the games anyway—

sometimes even Wayne and Wendell came, if they were caught up with the farm work. All Andy had to do was keep the equipment in good shape, make sure it was all collected again after each game, and bring a jug of water and some paper cups for the team, along with a sandwich for Lois to give her energy.

The first game of the season was Saturday afternoon, against the *Westgate Wildcats*. Andy climbed into the station wagon beside Lois and a pile of bats and gloves, and Mrs. Moller drove them into town to the lot on the other side of the Ruby Theater, where the old bleachers had been repainted.

As Lois jumped out of the car, the team swarmed around her, wanting to see the game schedule. Some of the girls picked up the bats and gave a few practice swings. Mother and Aunt Wanda found a sunny place on the bleachers to sit, and Andy put his water jug and cups on the first row. When the *Westgate Wildcats* arrived in two pickup trucks, the teams hooted at each other and the game began.

As Andy watched a *Wildcat* strike out, he thought, *I'll bet Mrs. Haynes is on the phone right now, calling Mr. Sudermann and talking it over.*

When the next girl went to bat, Andy imagined Mr. Sudermann looking worried.

And by the time the third girl picked up the bat, Andy was sure that on Monday morning Mrs. Haynes would stand in front of the class with a new envelope in her hand and say, "There's been a change. The *new* topic for this year's contest is . . ."

Aunt Bernadine came by at the end of the first inning and sat down beside Mother and Aunt Wanda.

The *Beagles* were pretty awesome, Andy had to admit. The girls were rather hefty, for one thing, and each of them, he guessed, weighed at least 140 pounds, with arms the size of cantaloupes. The pitcher, a pretty girl with red hair, was clearly the favorite, and a group of boys had come to watch her pitch.

"That a'way, Shirley!" they'd yell when the ball sailed directly over home plate and the batter missed.

Andy sat there happily in his red-and-white T-shirt with *Bucksville Beagles* on the back of it, thinking some more about the contest. Maybe the new topic would be to invent a team sport that you didn't have to play with a ball. Already his mind was at work, thinking of his first paragraph, then the second . . .

"More mayonnaise next time," Lois told him when she came to get her sandwich, and Andy said he'd remember.

The *Beagles* won, seven-to-four, and the girls went crazy, hugging each other and yelling and slapping their teammates on the back. Then they all trooped across the road to the Dairy Queen, and one of the boys had his arm around the pitcher.

After Andy had collected all the bats and gloves and put them in the station wagon, he went over to the Dairy

Queen too, and sat down on a bench between Aunt Bernadine and Mother to eat his cone.

"We've got to get more of the family out for the next game," Mother said. "Where's Jack? I thought he'd be here."

"Always up to something," Aunt Bernadine said. "I don't know what he's doing, but he says it's something to do with conservation."

Andy stopped licking his cone and stared straight ahead. His tongue felt cold, then his throat, then his stomach. That dirty, rotten sneak! Jack was going to break the boycott! He'd thought of an essay and hadn't told anyone what it was.

5

Burned to a Crisp

ANDY WAS SO ANGRY THAT HE WENT RIGHT TO THE phone when he got home to call Jack and tell him off. But Aunt Bernie must have got back first, because the Barths' line was busy, as usual.

When he turned around, he saw Wayne standing there in his overalls and boots, holding one of the newborn piglets that wasn't getting enough to eat. Andy started to tell him about Jack and the contest, but decided to save his steam for Jack—didn't want any little bit of anger to get away.

"Puniest one of the lot," Wayne was saying. "Like to get pneumonia if he don't sturdy up." He held the piglet under one arm while he filled a syringe with penicillin.

Andy dialed Jack's number again. Still busy.

Through the window he could see Mother and Aunt Wanda and Lois inspecting the buds on the apple tree. *Trees.* Even *that* would have made a better essay topic than conservation. *How many things can you do with a tree?* Mr. Sudermann could have asked them. Use it to grow fruit, use it for shade, climb it, decorate it, build a house in it, string a clothesline from it, get maple syrup from it, hang a swing from it, get nuts from it—the list was endless. Then there were all the things you could do with a tree once you chopped it down: make a canoe out of the trunk; saw it into lumber; use the stump for a table; use the branches for firewood . . . Andy would have won the contest hands down.

Thinking of firewood made him look at the piglet again. Despite the sun outdoors, the air still had a sharpness to it that made the kitchen feel inviting.

"Want me to set up the warming bed?" he asked, and Wayne nodded. Andy went out on the back porch and got the apple crate and old blanket that had held a weak lamb the month before when the ewes were birthing. Andy set it on the floor between the hot air register and the stove. He watched as his brother held the piglet upside down by one hind leg and injected the needle into its rump. The piglet gave a loud squeal and twisted about in Wayne's hand. Boy, what Andy would like to do to Jack! Lasso him up by one foot and dangle him from the old chestnut. That was *another* thing you could do with a tree. He dialed Jack's number again. Still busy.

There was already a solution of ground soybeans, minerals, and milk in the refrigerator, and Andy heated some in a pan, then poured it into a baby bottle. "Moller's Hospital," Mother always called her kitchen in springtime, when one or more baby animals had to be nursed for a week or so. If there wasn't a box of chicks chirping next to the heat register, there was usually a listless lamb or a kitten. Last year, before his old dog Moses had died, it had been the retriever that Andy had cared for on a blanket near the stove.

Wayne handed the piglet to Andy, and Andy sat down on a kitchen chair, holding the piglet between his knees, and fed it from the bottle. The piglet sucked eagerly, noisily, milk leaking out onto the fine white hairs of its chin.

You eat like a pig, Jack had told Andy the week before, and all the anger came flooding back. With one hand Andy reached for the wall phone and clumsily dialed the Barths' again. The phone rang once, then again.

"This call cannot be completed as dialed," a recorded voice said. "Please hang up and try again."

Andy slipped the phone back on the hook, sighed, and gave his attention to the pig.

Mother and Lois came in the back door with Aunt Wanda.

"Moller's Hospital, open for business," Mother said when she saw the piglet. And then, bending down, "Poor little fella."

"Got me a couple more out there I might have to bring in," Wayne said. "Wendell's checking them out."

"Well, you give me a clear place on the counter to start supper," Aunt Wanda said grumpily. "Men'll take over the barn and the kitchen too if you let 'em."

By the time the piglet had finished the bottle, Andy's anger had gone from white hot to cool blue. He decided not to call Jack—not to talk to him at all, in fact. Give him the old silent treatment and get the other kids in on it too. That was about the worst thing you could do to somebody: pretend he wasn't there.

The day was rapidly going downhill. It had started out nice enough, with the *Beagles* winning the ball game. But it wasn't enough, it seemed, that Andy had to find out about Jack breaking the boycott. When he came to supper that evening, Andy found a big square block of Aunt Wanda's Meatloaf Medley right there in the center of the table.

Andy cringed. You never knew what Aunt Wanda was going to put into meatloaf: stale bread crumbs, leftover oatmeal, dried-up cheese . . . And as though even the meatloaf wasn't enough, she had cooked some squash to go along with it.

"Have some squash, Andy, and pass it around," she said.

Andy reached for it slowly. Watching Aunt Wanda out of the corner of his eye, he quickly passed it on to Wendell when she wasn't looking.

"Have some squash," he said. Even its name was repulsive, like something you'd stepped on, maybe. Who was it that named vegetables, anyway? Okra sounded like something from the bottom of the ocean, and rutabaga sounded like a disease of the joints.

Aunt Wanda and Mother had been talking once, and Aunt Wanda had said that, just to spite her, Andy never liked anything she made.

"Now that's not true, Wanda, and you know it," Mother had said. "Nobody likes your chocolate cake better than Andy. But he's *always* been a finicky eater. Wouldn't eat meatloaf if the Good Lord came down from Heaven and made it Himself."

Finicky eater was one of those phrases that Andy didn't like either. It reminded him of some skinny kid with his nose in the air. Andy was husky and his back was broad, and he didn't see why anyone should worry about him. Put the right things on the table, and he'd eat everything in sight. Put a sausage pizza in front of him right now, in fact, and he'd eat the whole thing.

The trouble with Bucksville was that there was only one place to buy pizza and that was a pizza stand. Most farmers, when they wanted to eat, wanted to sit down while they did it. There were only two other restaurants in the whole business district: the Home-Style Restaurant, with the same kind of everyday food you'd find on your table at home, and the Soul Food Kitchen and Carry-Out. The year before Sam Hollins' family took it over, the little frame restaurant had been called the Wonton Carry-Out and featured egg rolls; the year before that it was the Harmony Health Hut, featuring beansprouts eleven different ways. The problem was, as Big Earl Moller put it, that when he'd been pitching hay all morning, then rode into town, he wanted something more than a couple of egg rolls or a plate of beansprouts. He wanted food that would stick to his ribs and see him through till supper time. From the looks of the food Sam Hollins brought to school each day in his lunch bucket, it sure seemed to Andy that soul food would have just that kind of sticking power.

"What's the brown stuff on top of the squash?" Andy's father was asking Aunt Wanda now from across the table.

"It's nutmeg, Earl, and that squash dish is another one of my new recipes," Aunt Wanda told him. "You know what I've a mind to do? I'm just waiting for that Soul Food Kitchen to close and then I just might open a restaurant there myself."

Andy almost dropped his fork. Wayne and Wendell began to smile.

"What're you going to call your restaurant?" Wendell asked her. "Wanda's Wonders?"

"Wonderful Wanda's Wicked Wonders," grinned Wayne. "What about that?"

Lois giggled.

Wicked Wanda's Weird and Watery Wonders, Andy thought, but he didn't dare say it out loud.

It was as though Aunt Wanda knew what he was thinking, however: "I'll have you know that people have paid good money just for my recipes alone," she said. "There was a woman in Waverly who offered me five dollars just for the secret of my Okra Surprise."

Andy almost gagged.

"But what makes you think the Soul Food Kitchen will go out of business?" Mother asked.

"They *all* do, Edna. You know that. First it was the Harmony Health Hut and then that China place. They don't seem to realize that we like good solid American food around here, nothing foreign."

Andy couldn't even chew. He could see it now, Aunt Wanda's menu: Okra Surprise, Squash Supreme, Meatloaf Medley, and Rhubarb Delight. On Mother's Day, when all the farmers took their wives to restaurants for dinner, they would have to eat Aunt Wanda's Squash Supreme instead of the chicken and biscuits that Andy enjoyed so much from Sam's lunch box. On Saturdays, when they went to town and wanted a quick meal out, they would have to choose between the Home-Style Restaurant, which had the same old tired things on the menu week after week, year after year, or Aunt Wanda's restaurant with her meatloaf and okra. Now Andy had *two* things to worry about: how to keep Jack from ending the boycott and how to keep the Soul Food Kitchen in business.

Just before he went to sleep that night, he had a comforting thought: it didn't matter *what* Jack was writing about for his essay, because when they all got to school on Monday, the essay topic would be changed. Andy was sure of it.

At ten-thirty the next morning, the family left for church, half of them in the station wagon, the others in Wendell's pickup truck.

It was a twenty-minute drive to church, first through Bucksville, then out into open country again.

The day was even sunnier than the one before, and it was warm inside the car where Andy sat. The car went down the two-lane road, straight as an arrow. Every farmhouse they passed along the way sat nestled in a clump of trees—rows of hickory, pine or poplar, arranged at right angles—protecting the house and barn from the northwest. Earl Moller made a left turn onto Orchard Lane and another into the church driveway.

Farmers stood outside the church, greeting each other, welcoming spring. Andy noticed the way the older girls eyed his two brothers. They looked like insurance men when they were all dressed up, Wayne in his blue suit, Wendell in his brown one, their hair all fluffed with the blow dryer, their nails clean.

Wayne wanted to buy a farm as soon as he could and get started raising hogs. Wendell wanted to go to college and get a degree in agricultural science. Sometimes they talked of living on the same farm together and sometimes they talked of living separately, side by side, the way Mother and Aunt Bernadine did.

"You'll live together until one of you finds a wife, that's what," Mother always told them. "No wife wants an extra man about the house to feed."

Lois, in her yellow dress and yellow shoes, was talking with some girls over on the steps, using her purse to show just how she had held the bat when she'd hit a home run. Andy looked around to see if Jack was there, but there was no sign of him yet. *Remember,* he told himself. *Not one word to Jack, no matter what! The silent treatment starts today.*

The organ began to play, and little groups moved toward the door. Andy followed his dad to the steps and had just started to go up when he heard the familiar sound of Uncle Delmar's old rattly sedan. It sounded even worse than usual, however, and when Andy turned to look, he saw smoke pouring out from under the hood as the sedan pulled into the driveway.

The car doors were opening and the Barths were leaping out even before the car squealed to a stop. While people stared, Uncle Delmar ran around to the front and opened the hood. A plume of smoke rose from the engine.

Aunt Bernadine gave a little shriek and backed away. Wendell had already run to the water faucet at the side of the building and was yelling for a bucket. Someone handed him a coffee mug to fill with water, someone else came running with a collection plate, and by the time a third man appeared with a bucket, the smoke was beginning to clear.

Aunt Bernadine leaned weakly against Mother.

"All the way here, I'm saying, 'What's that smell, Delmar?' And just as we're pulling into the church driveway, we saw the smoke."

Everyone crowded around the sedan. Inside the church, the organ music faltered, then played on, but the minister had come to the door to look out.

Then, in the middle of the crowd, Uncle Delmar held something up—something round and flat and black. "What's this?" he asked.

"Looks like a hamburger," said Wendell. "*Smells* like a hamburger."

At that moment, Andy caught sight of Jack, standing over next to the church, his face pale.

Still holding the meat between his finger and thumb, Uncle Delmar turned toward his wife. "Bernadine?" he said. "Did you know there were hamburgers on top of my engine?"

"On . . . on top of your engine?" gasped Aunt Bernie.

"Looks like somebody's lunch. There were two of 'em frying right there under the hood of my car."

"Only two of them?" said Jack. "I put three . . ." And suddenly, he stopped.

Everyone turned. Jack's face went from gray to red.

"It was an experiment!" he croaked. "For school! For the Roger B. Sudermann Contest . . . !"

Uncle Delmar moved through the crowd and dangled the burned burger in front of Jack's face.

"I didn't know they'd burn, Dad!" Jack pleaded. "I was just using my imagination like Mr. Sudermann said."

"Sudermann be hanged," said Uncle Delmar, and he threw the hamburger as far away as he could throw it. It was the first time in his life Andy had ever seen Uncle Delmar lose his temper with Jack.

Andy sat in a pew between Lois and Wendell and tried his best not to laugh. He was listening to the 23rd Psalm, but his mind was on hamburgers. Wouldn't he love to have had a picture of Jack's face to show on the bus the next morning? Wait till the others found out what Jack had been up to—the way he'd been going along all week not saying a word about the contest, but working on something nonetheless, just like the sneak he was.

When he wasn't thinking about telling the others, however, Andy was thinking something else: What kind of an experiment *was* it, anyway? What in the world did hamburgers have to do with conservation?

6

Astronauts and Grasshoppers

ANDY DIDN'T HAVE TO TELL ANYONE ON THE BUS THE next morning, because they'd all heard already. Anything that happened in Bucksville was usually broadcast from one end of town to the other within an hour or so, especially if Aunt Wanda or Aunt Bernadine got on the phone.

The minute Jack stepped on board, Russ called out, "Hey, Jack, how do you like your hamburgers?"

"Well done!" somebody else yelled from in back, and Jack flushed beet red.

Andy forgot all about the silent treatment. "You know what you are, Jack? A sneak," he said. "A dirty, rotten sneak, making us think you weren't going to enter the contest."

"I didn't say I *wasn't* going to enter it, did I?" Jack

asked, his voice a little shaky. "When Dora was going around asking everyone, she forgot to ask me."

Everyone looked at Dora. "I guess he was one of the ones I missed," she said.

"But you didn't say you *were* entering the contest, either," Russ said to Jack. "You heard us talking about a boycott. How come you didn't say anything then?"

"I didn't even get the idea until Friday!" Jack protested.

Somehow Andy believed him. "Oh, let him alone," he said to Russ. "Sneaks like to be alone anyway." It didn't make one bit of difference, because Mr. Sudermann would certainly have changed the topic by now.

"I'm not a sneak!" Jack said, and sat down in a seat behind the driver.

Andy was the first one off the bus and the first one inside the classroom. He hung up his jacket and walked toward his seat. Halfway there, however, he stopped. Slowly he turned his head toward the sign-up sheet on the bulletin board.

There was one name on it: Jack's. Jack must have signed the sheet just before he left for home over the weekend. With even one name on the list, Mrs. Haynes wouldn't have called Mr. Sudermann. The topic was still conservation. Russ and Dora stopped and stared at the sign-up sheet too, and Andy knew they were all thinking the same thing: Jack could win the contest just because no one else had entered.

They gave Jack the silent treatment all morning. Even at lunchtime, they pulled their chairs close together at one end of their table in the all-purpose room, and Jack ate by himself.

"What do you think he was trying to do with those hamburgers?" Russ asked at last.

"Burn up his dad's car, what else?" Dora said. The three of them laughed uneasily.

"So who cares, anyway?" said Andy.

"Yeah," said Russ. "Who cares?"

They all did, and Andy knew it.

Sam Hollins and his cousin Travers were handing out newly printed flyers that Sam's older brother Clay had designed, advertising the Soul Food Kitchen and Carry-Out. Clay was in business school, and he'd made the flyers as an assignment for a class in advertising:

<u>Two Meals for the Price of One!</u>

Bring a friend to Hollins' Soul Food Kitchen and Carry-Out and get one meal free!

Featuring: Southern fried chicken
Ham and red-eye gravy
Hush puppies
Collard greens
Black-eyed peas
Sweet potato pie and more!

We put the "soul" back into soul food!

Andy took a whole stack of the flyers and said he'd pass them around at church the next Sunday. "The library, too," he told Sam. "People always pass out things at the library."

"All right!" said Sam, pleased. And then, "Guess what I've got in my lunch. You guess it, you can have it."

"Chicken," Andy guessed.

"Wrong."

"Ham."

"What else?"

"Biscuits."

"What else?"

Andy studied the flyers from the Soul Food Kitchen. "I hope it's not collard greens. Collard sounds like somebody's uncle: Mr. Collard Green."

"You're weird, Andy," said Travers.

They sat out on the grass afterward, watching the sixth graders play soccer. Andy saw Jack sitting off by himself on the swings, twisting around and around on the wooden seat until the chains were one tightly twisted cord above him. Then he'd lift his feet and spin dizzily about in a circle, faster and faster, until finally the chains above jerked free. He was probably thinking of something else to put in his essay, Andy thought angrily. What in the *world* had Jack been trying to do with those hamburgers, anyway? He still couldn't figure it out.

When the bell rang at the end of recess, he and his

friends reluctantly gave up the warm April sunshine and sauntered slowly toward the door.

"You know," said Dora as they started up the steps, "if I *did* think of a good idea for the essay contest, I suppose I'd enter it. Now that Jack's broken the boycott, I mean."

Andy looked at her sideways as they went down the hall.

"I mean, I *don't* have an idea—conserving water or something—but if I *did,* well, I suppose I might want to try it. Wouldn't you?"

"I guess," said Andy.

He felt as though things were crumbling all around him. He tried to keep his mind on school that afternoon and avoided looking at Jack. The class was studying outer space in science class, and Russ was giving a report on astronauts. Russ *always* gave reports on astronauts. Even in history. Once, when they were supposed to give reports on famous artists of the past, Russ said that if rocket ships had been invented in 1490, the great artist Leonardo da Vinci would have been the first astronaut because it was da Vinci who made the first drawings of flying machines. Russ got a C on that report.

This time Russ was talking about the training that astronauts had to go through before they could go up in space. He said that they had to learn about survival in all different kinds of places, in case the rocket came down unexpectedly, and he told how astronauts learned to make shelters out of their rubber life rafts and to eat snakes and lizards. Andy's stomach seemed to wobble.

On the bus ride home that afternoon, Andy said, "I'll bet you made that up about astronauts eating snakes and lizards."

"I did not!" said Russ. "I read it in *National Geographic.*"

That settled it, then. *National Geographic* wouldn't lie. Andy felt depressed. He'd never wanted to be an astronaut, it's true, but he didn't particularly like to know that he *couldn't* be one if he wanted. He wouldn't make it to first base. He couldn't even get past collard greens and Aunt Wanda's Okra Surprise.

And then, for the final touches on an awful day, Russ said, "Don't be mad, Andy, but I think I've got an idea for an essay."

"Why should I be mad?" Andy asked hotly. "Jack's already broken the boycott."

"Well, then," said Russ, "do you know what happens to your garbage?"

Andy didn't think he could stand it. "No," he said, his voice flat.

"Trucks take it to a field north of Bucksville, and bulldozers plow it under. When that field is full, they go to some other place. When *all* the land around Bucksville is full of trash and garbage, what will we do then?"

"I don't know," said Andy. He didn't much care, either.

"I don't know either," Russ went on, "but in New York, boats take it out and dump it in the ocean. *Tons* of it. Every day!"

Andy frowned. He hadn't known that. He didn't much like the thought of garbage in the ocean, even though he'd never even *seen* an ocean.

"Pretty soon," said Russ, "the whole planet will be filled with garbage. So in my essay, I'm going to suggest that we conserve land by sending our garbage to outer space."

Andy turned and stared at him. Now he *really* couldn't believe it. Banana peels and Fruit Loops boxes and old rubber tires orbiting the earth forever? Or rocket ships, loaded with garbage, traveling to distant planets?

"Well," he said finally. "It's an idea, all right." Andy simply did not know what else to say.

By the time the bus let him off at the end of the drive, Andy was determined to enter the contest too. He would put his name on the sign-up sheet the next day. If Russ was going to write about sending garbage to outer space, then Andy could certainly think of *something*.

The first thing he always thought about when he got home from school, however, was food. Andy put his books on the kitchen table, picked up the saucer of cookies that Mother always left for him, and took them out onto the back steps.

He munched thoughtfully, letting the crumbs fall on the grass below. Russ was going to write about conserving land, so Andy didn't want to write about that. Dora Kray had already hinted that she might like to write about conserving water. The food supply? Whatever Jack had been doing with those hamburgers, he certainly wasn't conserving food. Maybe Andy could write about that. "How I Would Conserve the Food Supply: Keep Aunt Wanda From Opening a Restaurant," by Andy Moller.

He thought so hard his brain hurt. Fourteen things to do with a brick didn't help much here. To win Mr. Sudermann's contest, you really had to think up something far out. Mr. Sudermann wouldn't award a prize to an essay that just anyone might write. It had to be so unusual that there was "imagination" stamped all over it.

He wedged the toes of his sneakers beneath the log that lined Aunt Wanda's patch of rhubarb there by the back steps, lifting it slightly off the ground. A brown beetle moved along underneath and Andy kept the log up until the beetle had inched its way out and was making its way through the grass.

He was still feeling slightly sick from the thought of astronauts eating lizards. He wondered if he would *ever* be able to do such a thing. If he were on a desert island, for example, and starving, could he do it? He didn't even know that you *could* eat snakes and lizards without something awful happening to you.

One of the yellow cats walked over from the barn and rubbed up against Andy's legs. Suddenly its body tensed and it stood motionless, watching the beetle crawl through the grass. The beetle stopped, deciding which way to go. The cat dropped to its belly, muscles quivering.

"Don't even think it," Andy said to the cat.

Just then the beetle moved and the cat pounced. It grabbed the beetle in its paws. Crunch. Smack. The cat's jaws moved. One of the beetle's legs hung out one side of the cat's mouth.

Andy put his head down between his knees and sucked in his cheeks. Now he *knew* he was going to get sick. But he didn't. He got a terrific idea instead.

7

~~~~~~~~~~~~~~~~~~~~~~~~~~~~~~~~

Bon Appetit!

THE WAY ANDY FIGURED IT WAS THIS: IF THE POPULA-
tion ever grew so big that there wasn't enough food to feed
everybody, then people could save their lives by eating
things they hadn't thought of eating before. Things like
lizards and snakes and grasshoppers. Not that *Andy*
would eat them, of course, but some day, if people were
starving, *somebody* might.

*Start with what you have and see how far you can
stretch it,* Mr. Sudermann had said. *Put your imaginations
to work.* Maybe you didn't have to be starving. Maybe, if
you were just poor or you wanted to save money on your
grocery bill, you could find stuff to eat in your own backyard.

Andy knew that primitive tribes ate things like grubs,

which was just like eating worms. He had heard about fancy stores selling chocolate-covered ants as a novelty item. But no one he knew, except the yellow cat, had ever made a meal out of beetles. The first thing he had to do was find out exactly what could be eaten safely. Wendell had told him once that a university was a place where you could find out anything you wanted to know, so Andy wrote a letter to Iowa State University:

> Dear Sir:
> I am writing an essay for a contest
> and I need to know what bugs and
> things you can eat. And worms too.
> How do you know if they are poison or
> not? How do you fix them? Please
> answer soon.
>
> > Yours truly,
> > Andy Moller

On the envelope he wrote, "Department of Bugs," and then he added the address he had copied from the catalog in Wendell's room, with his own address in the corner.

Aunt Wanda saw him putting on the stamp.

"Who's the letter to?" she asked, as she carried her jade plant to a sunny place on the window ledge.

"Oh, somebody," Andy told her.

"Well, most letters *are* to somebody," she said, and cast him a strange look.

Andy walked down to the end of the lane toward the mailbox. He was remembering once when he was about six years old, walking to the mailbox with Jack. Andy had been afraid of the Moller's turkey then—a big tom turkey which would suddenly take a dislike to you and come flapping and gobbling over to peck at your heels. For a while Andy had never gone outside unless the turkey was in its pen, but on that particular day, Jack had been visiting and told Andy that the turkey was locked up when it wasn't. They'd gotten only halfway down the drive to the mailbox when there came the old tom. Jack had laughed and climbed up a plum tree, but the turkey had chased Andy screaming back to the house, pecking at him all the way.

And what had Aunt Bernie said?

"Look how my Jack can climb!" That's what she'd said. She was always comparing the boys, and it was always Jack who came out ahead.

Andy put the envelope in the mailbox and raised the red flag so the mailman would know that there was a letter to be collected. Later, when he was doing his homework on the sunporch and had come into the dining room to get an eraser, he'd heard Aunt Wanda and Mother talking about him in the kitchen.

"Of course I'm not going to ask him who that letter

was to, and don't you go peeking in the mailbox, either," Mother was saying. "It's his business, after all."

"Well, who does he know he has to write a letter to, that he can't call up on the phone?" Aunt Wanda went on. "He's in a bit of trouble, if you ask me. Was caught taking something from the five-and-dime, I'll bet, and he's got to pay it back."

"Why on earth would you think a thing like that?" Mother demanded. "If you ask me, he's got a girl somewhere. That's the likeliest reason for a letter that I can think of."

For crying out loud! Andy said to himself, and went back out on the sunporch.

By the end of April, at least nine fifth graders had broken the boycott and were trying out for the contest. Dora Kray had rigged up some kind of funnel contraption on the roof of the Krays' garage to collect rainwater as a conservation measure. Andy thought this was probably the best idea anyone had thought of so far, until Mother told him that when she was a girl, they *always* collected water in a rain barrel, and used it to wash their hair. Russ, of course, to conserve land, was still trying to figure out a way to send garbage to outer space, but no one could figure out what Jack was trying to conserve.

On May 1, when Andy had about given up ever hearing from the University, there was a letter for him in the box, and he was glad he had found it before anyone else did:

Dear Andy:

Your letter asking about bugs and things has been given to me for reply, and I hope I will be able to help. Probably most insects are edible, especially their larvae or pupae. But because some of them—especially brightly-colored insects—might have poisons in their bodies, it would be best to stick with crickets, grasshoppers, and ordinary brown beetles.

Ant and bee larvae are also a good source of fat and protein; meal worms, often found where grain is stored, are delicious, I understand, fried in garlic butter. To prepare insects for eating, put them on a diet of cornmeal for a few days to rid their digestive tracts of grit, then cook. Earthworms can also be put on a diet of applesauce, then simmered until tender. Grasshoppers, crickets, and beetles, lightly toasted, with the legs and wings removed, add crunch to a recipe, and can be used in place of nuts for brownies.

If you don't like the idea of dropping live worms and insects in boiling water, you might put them in a covered box in the freezer first, then cook them later. Good luck on your essay, and *bon appetit!*

Cordially,
John Burrows, Entomologist

Andy understood the whole letter except the last two words before "cordially."

"Mom," he said that evening as he worked his arithmetic problems on the kitchen table, and she sat across from him going over her poultry and egg records, "What does *bon appetit* mean?"

"*Bon appetit?*" Mother looked up. "It's French, Andy. It means 'good appetite' or 'good eating.' 'Enjoy your meal'—something like that."

Andy kept one hand tightly over his mouth and said nothing.

8

One-half Cup of Nuts

ON SATURDAY, EARL MOLLER WENT INTO TOWN FOR A new auger motor for the silo, and took Andy with him. When they passed the Barths' farm, with its L-shaped patch of trees around the house, Andy asked, "How's Uncle Delmar's car doing? Did Jack's hamburgers hurt it any?"

"Another minute or so and they might have, but Del got the blamed things off in time," his father said. "Jack won't be trying that again soon, I can tell you." He looked at Andy and pushed back his cap, the one with the *Farley's Feed* emblem in front, two overlapping red F's against a white background. Almost all the men in Bucksville wore a cap from Farley's, except that the young farmers, like Wayne, wore the bill around in back instead. "How's *your* essay coming? You going to enter the contest too?"

"I'm thinking of it," Andy told him.

"Well, don't you go cooking lunch under *my* hood, or I'll set fire to your britches," Earl said with a smile.

The reason Andy couldn't tell his family what his essay was about was because, after he'd learned to cook the stuff he collected, he'd need somebody to taste it. He could just imagine what Lois would say if he asked her.

Are you nuts? That's what Lois would say.

He also had to find some recipes. He knew just what Aunt Wanda would say if he asked her how you fry meal worms in garlic butter.

You don't, she'd say. *Not in my skillets, you don't.*

After they bought the motor and Andy got some more three-ring notebook paper and a magic marker, Earl said, "You want to pick up a couple sandwiches somewhere?"

That's when Andy remembered the flyer from the Soul Food Kitchen and Carry-Out. He fished it out of his back pocket. "Two meals for the price of one, Dad," he said.

Mr. Moller's eyes scanned the menu there on the advertisement. "Looks pretty good to me," he said, and they drove down Main to North Street and to the little yellow frame building on the corner.

Soul Food Kitchen and Carry-Out, said a sign above the door, showing a smiling chicken at one end of the sign and a thick piece of pie at the other.

The first thing Andy saw in the little room with its green tables and yellow linoleum was Sam, who was putting silverware on the tables.

"Hi!" he called out when he saw Andy. He showed them to a little table by the wall and stood off to one side grinning while Mrs. Hollins came over to take their orders. She was a thin woman in a white uniform and white shoes with thick soles, and had a smile that stretched across her face, just like Sam's.

"How you doing?" she asked, and looked down at Andy. "You and Sam know each other from school?"

Andy nodded.

There was a sign above the grill that said, *Ask about our daily special.*

"What about the daily special?" Andy's father asked.

Mrs. Hollins smiled even wider. "Well, you are *some* kind of lucky today, because the special for Saturdays is catfish, all you can eat."

Andy's heart sank. Why couldn't it have been fried chicken or hot dogs or chili or hamburgers? "Catfish" sounded too much like "cat food" or "dog biscuits" or something.

"You order a Saturday special," Sam's mother went on, "and you get a plate of catfish, hush puppies, turnip greens, cornbread, and a big piece of rhubarb pie. All you can eat. You order a Saturday special, you won't want *anything* till Sunday noon."

She laughed and Earl laughed and Sam's father over by the grill laughed too.

Andy's father pulled out the "two-for-the-price-of-one" flyer that Andy had shown him.

"That's right," said Sam's mother. "Neither *one* of you is going to want anything at all till church is over on Sunday."

"Could I . . . have chicken instead?" Andy asked.

"Of *course* you can have chicken," said Mrs. Hollins, as though it were the most reasonable request in the world. She didn't glare down at him as Aunt Wanda would have done and screech, "You don't like my *catfish?*"

"One Saturday special and one chicken platter," she called to her husband, and soon the little restaurant was filled with spicy smells and the sound of grease bubbling in the deep-fryer behind the counter.

"Ahhh!" said Earl, when the dinners arrived. As Mrs. Hollins poured more coffee in his cup, he said, "How's business?"

"Well, now that we put out those flyers, it's picking up some," Sam's mother told him. "Our older boy, Clay, is in business school, and we get a lot of good ideas from him. When he graduates he's going to help run the restaurant. Last year, when we first started, I wasn't sure how long there was going to *be* a restaurant, but now I think we're doing okay."

The way Earl tore into that catfish, shaking his head and smacking his lips, Andy knew it must taste pretty good. The chicken was good too. Aunt Wanda's chicken had never tasted this good. Not even Aunt Bernie's or Mother's. Andy grinned at Sam, who was watching them over by the counter.

What he was really thinking about, however, was earthworms, and whether they could be rolled in the Hollins' specially-flavored cornmeal and fried in hot grease. That would make one recipe for his essay.

After church on Sunday, when his chores were done, Andy spent the afternoon turning over logs to look for beetles. He worked until he had filled half a jar and took them up to his room, tucked inside his shirt. He put them in the little screened cage that he once used for his hamster, and carefully poured a small pile of cornmeal at one end.

For three days, Andy checked the cage, cleaning out the bottom and putting in fresh cornmeal. The brown beetles, looking fat and healthy, climbed up on each other's backs to get at the cornmeal. At the end of four days, Andy put the beetles in a small cookie tin with a tight lid and took it to the big freezer chest in the basement. He stuck it down in one corner beneath a stack of his mother's apple pies.

Saturday morning he checked again. The beetles were frozen solid. Some were on their backs with their legs in the air. Others looked as though they had frozen standing up. Andy peeled off all the wings and legs and threw them away, then chopped up the bodies into pieces until the little pile looked like a cup of black walnuts. Andy didn't mind this part. He didn't mind baiting a hook when he went fishing, either. It was the thought of eating the things that made his tongue curl. He simply did not allow himself to think about it, however. And everytime his *throat* started to think about it, Andy told himself that only a far-out essay like this would win the contest. He put the beetles in a pan and toasted them in the oven for five minutes, then put them back in the jar. They gave off a sharp, pungent odor, and Andy kept the windows open while they were toasting.

"I want to make some brownies to take to school on Monday," he told his mother. "You give me the recipe, I'll make them myself."

"Now that's an offer I can't refuse," Mother told him. She took a recipe card from her box and showed him where she kept the flour and cocoa.

"He's got a girl, I'm sure of it," Andy heard her say to Aunt Wanda out on the sunporch. "Can't think of any other reason he'd be wanting to take brownies to school."

The batter was dark and moist. When the flour and eggs and sugar had been mixed, Andy put in a quarter of a cup of chopped walnuts and then, his teeth clenched, a quarter of a cup of chopped beetle.

All the time the brownies were baking, Andy wondered if he could smell the beetles. When the brownies were done, he took them out, cooled them for twenty minutes, then cut them into squares and piled them onto a platter. He was just washing out the bowl and spoon in the sink when Wendell came into the kitchen, a screwdriver hanging out of one pocket.

"Need me a 3/8-inch screw with a flat head," he said, rummaging around in the big drawer near the stove where Mother said you could find anything from toothpicks to flashlights. And then Wendell saw the brownies.

"Hey!" he said. "Don't mind if I do!" And he reached out one big hand, picked up a thick brownie, and took a bite.

Andy stood over by the wall, scarcely breathing. He saw Wendell's jaws go up and down, saw him swallow. Then another bite. Crunch. The jaws were moving again. Wendell held the brownie out in front of him, turning it around and around in his hand while he chewed, looking at it from all angles, then swallowed once more and popped the rest of it in his mouth.

"Good!" he said, wiping his hand on his jeans.

Andy silently collapsed in a chair by the table, his stomach queasy, but his heart pounding with relief.

9

Cooking with Steam

ON MONDAY, AS SOON AS ANDY GOT TO SCHOOL, HE took Sam Hollins aside in the coatroom.

"Guess what I've got in my lunch," he said.

"Roast beef," said Sam.

"No. Listen, Sam, don't tell *anybody,* not even Travers. It's brownies."

"What's so secret about brownies? Let me taste one."

"You wouldn't want any."

The bell rang just then and Sam looked at Andy strangely. "*Why* wouldn't I want any?"

Andy whispered in his ear. "They've got chopped-up beetles in them."

Sam backed away as though Andy had slipped a beetle on him. "Why'd you do that?"

"Look, it's for the contest, and I want you to help me. I wrote to a man at the University and he says you can eat worms and beetles and things if you fix them right, and he told me how. It's to save the food supply."

"You're going to save it maybe, not me," said Sam.

"You don't have to eat them. Just don't tell anyone else, okay? I've got to see if they're any good." Just because Wendell would eat anything didn't mean that anyone else would.

"So what do you want me to do?"

Andy waited until Russ had gone on by, then whispered again: "I've got to figure out some more recipes," he said. "I'll talk to you later."

The morning seemed to drag along. Every time Andy looked at the clock, certain that at least fifteen minutes had passed, only five minutes had gone by.

Finally it was noon, and the fourth, fifth, and sixth graders noisily took their lunch boxes from the coatroom and went racing down the hall to the all-purpose room.

"Just act natural," Andy told Sam. "Don't say *anything*. Don't even look at the brownies—your face will give it away." He and Sam sat down at the fifth-grade table and soon Russ and Dora and the others came over.

"Hey! Look what I've got in my lunch! A whole stack of brownies!" Andy said, as if in surprise. "Anybody want one?"

In answer, seven or eight hands reached over and grabbed at the chocolate squares. In a few seconds they were all gone. There wasn't even one left for Andy. The others laughed. So did Andy.

"That's okay," he said, "I've got more at home."

Across the table, Sam was looking very strange, because he was trying so hard not to. He was especially trying not to look at the brownies, and when his eyes were about to fall on one, he would suddenly turn the other way. Once, when the cuff of somebody's sleeve touched his hand, Sam jerked his arm away as though a beetle had just crawled up on it. Andy frowned.

Down at the far end of the table, Jack was eating by himself again.

"Hey, Russ, you took two brownies," Andy said. "Give one to Jack."

Jack looked up in surprise.

"Take it," said Russ, and slid one of his brownies down the formica table toward Jack. It hit the edge of someone's thermos bottle and broke in half. Out fell what Andy knew for certain was a piece of a beetle's back. Jack picked up the beetle back, popped it in his mouth, and followed it with a bite of the brownie. "Thanks, Andy," he said.

Sam closed his eyes. Andy, himself, felt for a moment that he was going to be sick. It was as though the beetle were in *his* mouth, on *his* tongue . . .

The talk turned to the contest again. Russ said that he was having a little trouble figuring out how to get the garbage *ready* for outer space. Two others said that their essays were almost ready to turn in. Just then Travers came over from the sixth-grade table. He saw the brownies sitting there on the table and grabbed Dora Kray's.

"Give that back!" Dora told him, reaching for it, but Travers laughed and took a big bite.

"Yuk!" he said, and Andy's heart sank.

Travers spit out the bite into his hand and stared at it. "It's got *nuts* in it! I *hate* nuts!" he said.

Andy watched Travers picking all the pieces of nuts and beetles out of the brownie and dropping them on the floor.

"Oh, just *eat* it, man, for Pete's sake!" Sam told him. Travers stuck the remains of the brownie in his mouth. Crunch. Smack. Sam closed his eyes again, and Andy's stomach lurched. But at least Andy knew that you could use beetles in brownies and no one would know the difference. Now he had at least one recipe to use in his essay.

"Listen," Sam said to Andy after they went outdoors. "How do you know it won't hurt him?"

"The man from the University said it wouldn't. I sterilized them first. I'm doing worms next."

"Don't you give any to me!"

"*You* don't have to eat any, Sam! But you know the way your dad fried that chicken and catfish? If I got you some worms, all cleaned and dead and everything, would you get them fried for me, without him knowing?"

"You *mean* it!" Sam said.

"Please!"

"I'll think about it," Sam told him.

When Andy got off the bus that afternoon, he found Mother and Aunt Wanda getting ready to go over to Uncle Delmar and Aunt Bernadine's for dinner.

"Delmar's plowing up his bottom land for wheat this year, and Earl and Wayne and Wendell are over there now helping fertilize it," Mother told him. "We'll be eating there tonight. You can ride over with us now or wait and walk with Lois. Someone's driving her home from cheerleading practice."

Andy didn't especially want to go to the Barths' early, but he didn't really feel like walking either, so he decided to ride along. Maybe, instead of hanging around the house with Jack, he could go out in the field with Wayne and Wendell till suppertime. So he climbed in the back seat of the station wagon, beside a cardboard box filled with a coconut cake, a dish of scalloped potatoes, some creamed corn, and a home-baked loaf of rye bread.

When they got to the Barths' farmhouse, Jack's bicycle was resting against a tree. Andy remembered how Jack used to try to run him down with it—chase him all around the yard. Andy had complained to his mother about it but it had been no use.

"I think the boy is lonely," Mother had said. "People don't act that way unless they need attention."

Lonely! Attention!

"Aunt Bernie and Uncle Delmar give him so much attention he's about to drown in it," Andy had told her.

"And that's just it. They've made it hard for him to get along with other people. It's friends his own age he really needs."

"Poor baby!" said Andy, without one bit of sympathy.

Now he carried the box inside for Mother while Aunt Wanda held open the door to the side porch. The Barths' porch was, in Aunt Wanda's words, "A living pigsty, and I don't care if Bernadine *is* my sister!"

Andy never thought of it as a pigsty. It was pretty interesting, in fact, because you never knew what you'd find. All along one wall hung coats and flannel shirts, and a huge mound of sneakers sat beneath them—all kinds, all sizes, mixed up together. There was an old broken rocker, a table with only three legs, dusty flower pots with dead plants in them, an empty bread box, feed sacks, a basket of walnuts, and snow tires for the sedan.

"Lord have mercy," Aunt Wanda breathed as she tripped over a green Converse high-top and moved resolutely on inside.

Aunt Bernadine was making chicken and dumplings for supper, which Andy liked, and Jack was nowhere in sight. Maybe this was his lucky day after all. Andy set the box on the table, then went back out to see whether he could tell where Uncle Delmar and his father and brothers were working. They weren't in sight either, and Andy wasn't sure he wanted to go looking for them. He walked back through the kitchen and turned on the TV in the living room while his mother and aunts discussed whether they should slow-cook the beans in salt pork or steam them with onions.

There wasn't much on TV but "Mister Rogers". Andy almost preferred having Jack around. It was strange, but when Jack was there to bother him, Andy really hated his guts, but when he wasn't around, Andy missed him in a weird sort of way.

"Andy," Aunt Bernie called, "Jack disappeared the minute he got home from school and never did finish mowing the grass in the side yard. Find him for me, would you, and tell him to get it done?"

Andy smiled to himself. *With pleasure.*

He went upstairs and down the hall to Jack's room. The door was closed. Andy tapped on the door. "Jack?" he said, and waited. No answer. He tapped again. "Jack?" he called, a little louder. Still no answer.

This is a trick, he thought. *Jack's got me all set up to open the door.*

Slowly he turned the handle, then kicked open the door with his foot. Nothing happened. No bucket of water from above. No tower of tin cans behind the door.

The room, however, was filled with steam. Even the windows were steamed over.

Andy went in and looked around. Jack wasn't there. A vaporizer was going on the top of his dresser, however, spraying a cloud of steam toward the ceiling.

Andy stared at the vaporizer. There was a strange

rattling sound inside it. Curious, Andy lifted the top and saw a pyrex jar bouncing around in the boiling water. Andy unplugged the vaporizer and let the water settle down for a minute. Then he picked up an old T-shirt of Jack's and lifted the jar out. It looked like cocoa there inside it. He set the jar down carefully on Jack's dresser, unscrewed the lid, and sniffed. It *smelled* like cocoa.

Andy put the jar back inside and placed the top on the vaporizer again. What the heck was Jack doing for his essay, anyway? Hamburgers on the engine of a car; cocoa in a vaporizer. Andy could hardly stand not knowing. Whatever Jack was on to, it was far-out, all right.

Andy went back downstairs and outside, circled the silo, then walked through the open doors of the barn. There were soft sounds coming from the harness room on the left, and Andy stopped.

Jack was standing there with his back to Andy, humming to himself and ironing! Andy stared. On the workbench was Aunt Bernie's steam iron and a loaf of bread. Andy couldn't see what else, but after Jack set the iron down, he turned something over, picked up the iron again, and ironed some more.

Andy walked in. "Hi, Jack," he said.

Jack almost dropped the iron. He managed to set it up on its end, then quickly spread his hands out over a piece of brown wrapping paper on the workbench, as though to hide it.

"What are you doing?" Andy asked.

"Just get out of here, snot-nose," Jack said. "What are *you* doing here?"

"We're here for supper," Andy told him. "Your mom wants you to finish mowing the grass." All the time Andy was talking, he was trying to figure out what Jack had been ironing. He could see something white and something yellow beneath the wrapping paper. He sniffed the air, and then he was sure of it: a cheese sandwich! Jack was making a grilled-cheese sandwich between two pieces of brown paper.

"Okay, but you just get out," Jack told him. "This isn't any of your business. You're just trying to steal my idea."

"Why would I want *your* idea? I've got one of my own," Andy said. He turned and walked out of the barn.

"And stay out of my room, too!" Jack yelled after him.

"Too late!" Andy called, laughing. "Boy, that cocoa sure was good!"

All through supper, Jack glared at Andy and Andy glared back.

"What'd you fellas do—have another fight?" Earl Moller said as he helped himself to the creamed corn. "Never saw two cousins in my life who got along worse than you do."

"A sin and a shame!" said Aunt Wanda reproachfully. "You boys don't quit scowling at each other, you can just forget about my coconut cake."

Andy didn't care one bit. Coconut was way down the list somewhere along with sweet potatoes and squash.

"Say, Wanda, what's this I hear about you maybe starting a restaurant?" Uncle Delmar asked.

"If that Soul Food Kitchen goes out of business, I just might," she said.

"Well, I don't know now," said Andy's father. "Andy and I had lunch there the other day and I don't think I ever had a piece of fried catfish or a biscuit that tasted as good as that."

"You never had catfish before in your life, Earl, that's why," said Mother. She seemed a little upset herself. When you got to comparing biscuits, even Mother got edgy.

"Well, it sure was good."

"Wanda, you don't know the first thing about running a business," said Aunt Bernie. "What makes you think you could?"

Now the temperature in the room was heating up fast. The looks that passed between Andy and Jack were nothing compared to the looks that went across the table between Aunt Wanda and Aunt Bernadine.

"Well, I could do a lot better than a bunch of foreigners," Aunt Wanda sputtered, and Wayne and Wendell whooped with laughter.

"That means anyone born outside Fayette County," said Wayne.

"What do you mean?" asked Wendell, a grin a foot

wide on his face. "Fayette County's a big place. Anyone born outside Bucksville's a foreigner, now *you* know that!"

Aunt Wanda sniffed indignantly. "Well, those hippies who ran the Harmony Health Hut didn't make it, and the Chinese didn't either. I'm not wishing bad luck on anyone, mind you, but if the Soul Food Kitchen goes out of business, that's as good a place as any to serve my Okra Surprise."

Andy concentrated on keeping his creamed corn on one side of his plate and his scalloped potatoes on the other. He didn't much care if Aunt Wanda took out after Bernie, but he didn't want her talking about folks she didn't even know. If Aunt Wanda set her mind on closing that restaurant, she could do it just by getting on the phone and talking it down. The only solution, as Andy saw it, was to get her to know and like Sam Hollins, and that evening, Andy asked if he could invite Sam over.

"Certainly," Mother said. "And ask him to bring that biscuit recipe with him."

10

Capturing the Cow

ANDY AND SAM MADE AN AGREEMENT. SAM WOULD come home with Andy one afternoon and spend the night. The next day Andy would stay overnight with him, and somehow they would cook the worms. Andy had taken a quart of Aunt Wanda's applesauce from the basement and poured it into an old wash basin for his worm colony, hiding it under his bed. He told Sam about it at school and promised to show him when he came over.

"What'll she say when she finds out you got worms in her applesauce?" Sam asked.

"Same thing your dad would say if he knew we were going to cook them in his deep fryer," Andy told him.

"You're lucky *I* didn't enter the contest," Sam said. "I'd burn those worms to little bits."

The day that Sam came home with Andy, Aunt Wanda was at her worst. She met them at the door without a word of welcome to Sam, and announced that Mrs. Kray had just called to say that one of the heifers was loose and walking down the road.

"Where's Dad?" Andy asked.

"Out in the west field, and Wayne and Wendell are in a wrestling meet at the high school. Your mother's gone to pick up Lois from cheerleading practice."

Andy knew that Wayne and Wendell would be along shortly, and they were a lot more experienced at cow catching than he was, especially if that cow was She-girl, which he strongly suspected it was. He started to go on inside when he heard Sam say, "Guess we'll have to go catch that cow ourselves."

Andy turned and looked at him. He didn't *want* to go cow chasing right now; he wanted a handful of cookies; he wanted to show Sam the barn and the worms, and to talk about tomorrow night. With Jack so far along on his essay, there was no time to waste.

One look at Sam's eyes, however, and he knew his friend wanted to see what cow catching was all about; if Andy expected to get his worms deep-fried at Sam's place, they'd have to give it a try. One look at Aunt Wanda's eyes, and Andy knew they'd better catch that cow, even if it *was* She-girl.

He sighed. "All right," he said, putting his books on the step.

"Must have got through that weak place where our fence meets the Krays'," Aunt Wanda called after them. "I've been telling your father a cow's going to get through there if he doesn't fix it."

Andy got a rope from the shed and they started off. He wondered if Sam knew what they were in for. Wondered if he'd ever lived on a farm.

"Where'd you live before you moved to Bucksville?" he asked, when they reached the end of the lane and turned down the road toward the Krays'.

"Missouri," Sam told him. "St. Louis."

"How come you moved here?"

"Travers' dad wrote that there was a restaurant going out of business that we might be able to buy cheap. My folks always wanted their own restaurant. We worked one in St. Louis, but it wasn't ours."

"You like it in Bucksville?"

"I sure wouldn't mind living on a farm like *this!*" Sam said. Andy began to wish the afternoon would be a little more exciting than cow catching usually was.

About a quarter-mile down the road, Andy saw the heifer clamber up from the ditch and lope along the shoulder of the road.

"There she is," he said, but he wasn't sure if the heifer was coming toward them or moving away. He broke into a run. The animal lumbered out into the middle of the road, and now Andy could tell that she was moving away from them. The harder he and Sam ran, the faster the heifer went, her legs flying out at the sides like paddles. There was no doubt about it, it was She-girl, the most stubborn cow in the state of Iowa.

Andy skidded and pulled Sam to a stop beside him. "She'll run all the way to West Union if we chase her," he said. "We've got to sneak up on her from the side."

They both stood still on the asphalt. It didn't seem as though She-girl would ever stop running, but finally she slowed, and Andy was dismayed to discover that she was even further away from them now than she had been before. They started out again, Andy far over on one side of the road, Sam on the other, walking slowly and stopping every few minutes so the heifer wouldn't run again.

And then Andy saw a car coming toward them off in the distance, the Mollers' station wagon.

"That's Mom," he told Sam as the car came closer and stopped. A door opened on the passenger side and Lois jumped out.

"This one of ours?" she yelled.

"Yes!" Andy yelled back. "Got through the fence near the Krays'."

He saw Lois stick her head back in the car for a moment. Then she shut the door and began walking toward She-girl. The station wagon began moving forward slowly.

"They're going to try to herd her back home with the car," Andy said.

"Oh, shoot!" said Sam, disappointed.

She-girl stood still, facing the oncoming car, her tail swishing from side to side. The station wagon stopped, then inched forward again. The heifer didn't move. Mrs. Moller came within a few yards of She-girl, then a few feet, as Andy and Sam came up from behind. Lois waved her arms and shouted. Still the heifer didn't budge. The car stopped.

"Stupid cow!" Lois bellowed. "Shoo! Turn around! Get moving!"

The heifer's tail swished again.

Mother tapped the horn lightly, then tapped it again. The heifer remained standing. Mother honked once more, a long blast this time.

Before anyone knew what had happened, She-girl swung about, plunged down into the ditch alongside the road, and began munching the clover.

"*Mo*-ther!" Lois wailed. "It'll take all night to get her out of there!"

"Sam, this is my sister Lois," Andy said and then, as Mrs. Moller got out of the car, "and that's Mom."

"Hi, Sam," Mother said. "This *would* have to happen the day you came home with Andy. I guess I shouldn't have leaned on the horn."

Sam didn't look disappointed at all. He obviously was having a great time.

"Let's try the rope," Andy said, and he made his way sideways down the hill to the ditch, Sam following. Lois stood up on the road, hands on her hips, the green-and-white skirt of her cheerleading outfit whipping in the breeze.

Andy had never tried to move a cow before without his father's help, but he'd seen the way Wayne and Wendell did it. He handed one end of the rope to Sam and told him to hold it tightly. Then he went around behind She-girl, pulling the rope up against the heifer's hindquarters, and moved up along the other side. Now both he and Sam were standing in front of She-girl, one on either side, and the rope was stretched tightly behind the heifer's back legs.

"Go, She-girl," Andy said, taking a step forward and pulling on the rope. Sam did the same, moving forward every time Andy took a step, gripping the rope tightly. The heifer took a step or two and then stopped, and proceeded to eat the clover.

Sometimes, just by pulling on a rope, Wayne and Wendell could get a cow to move along. It was easier than pushing from behind and safer, too, in case the cow decided to kick.

Lois came scrabbling disgustedly down into the ditch and ran alongside the heifer, trying to get her to go up the bank. The heifer merely looked at her, twitched her ears, and began eating some more.

Lois threw back her head and wailed. "I am never going to live on a farm again if I have to live in the street! We are going to be in this ditch the rest of our natural lives!"

"Lois, hush up and *do* something!" said Mother. "If you're going to bellow, at least bellow at the cow." She picked up a small stone in the road and tossed it toward the heifer's feet. "Go!" she commanded, but She-girl didn't move.

Andy was trying not to laugh. Sam hardly knew what to watch, the heifer or Lois or Mother.

Lois went back up to the car and got her big green pompons. Then she climbed back down the bank again, waved them in the heifer's face, and hit her on the side of the head. Andy swallowed a giggle. Lois looked like she was teaching She-girl a new cheer.

The heifer herself was getting annoyed. Inch by inch they all moved up the slope. She-girl would go two feet forward, then drop one foot back.

Lois switched her on the hindquarters with her pompons, then picked up a stick.

"*Move,* you stubborn thing!" she commanded, and switched even harder. "*Move!*"

The heifer bolted forward, her front legs buckling as she climbed the bank, and finally she was on the road once more. Andy and Sam moved quickly up in front of her again, still keeping the rope taut to guide her straight ahead. Lois ran alongside, switching the heifer with her pompons, and Mother got back in the car and began moving slowly behind her.

It took about twenty-five minutes of stopping and starting to get as far as the Mollers' driveway, and Andy was afraid that the heifer would bolt and go on by. Just then, however, he saw Wendell's pickup coming from the other direction and a few seconds later the pickup was blocking the road from in front, the station wagon was blocking the road from behind, Andy and Sam were pulling on the rope stretched around She-girl's hind legs, and Lois was waving her pompons. The heifer decided she had had enough, turned suddenly, and went running as fast as she could go up the driveway toward the barn.

Wayne and Wendell couldn't stop laughing. They spilled out of the pickup, and stood leaning against each other in the road, whooping and holding their sides. Lois marched on into the house in a huff, and Andy put the heifer back in the barn.

"That," he said to Sam, "was cow catching." *Now* maybe Aunt Wanda would let them inside and they could make plans for the following day.

11

Applesauce

SAM DIDN'T WANT TO TALK ABOUT WORMS JUST YET,
however. He seemed to like everything he saw at the Mollers'. He and Andy climbed up the bales of hay in the barn
until they reached the window at the top and could see far
out over the landscape, even beyond the Krays'. They
chased each other around for a while, leaping from bale
to bale, and finally lay on their backs in the clean straw
of the spreader, and watched the swallows fly in and out
the high window, building nests in the rafters.

As the family gathered later in the kitchen for supper,
there was a lot of laughter over She-girl.

"I sure would've liked to have had a picture of you
coming down the road," said Wendell. "Andy and Sam
pulling from in front, Mom bringing up the rear, and Lois

in her cheerleading costume, waving the heifer on. . . ."
He laughed again.

Lois, who had changed into jeans, had to work to keep back a smile herself as she pulled out her chair at the table and plopped down in it. "Wouldn't care if I never saw another cow as long as I live," she said.

Aunt Wanda, however, was being only lukewarm nice, and when Andy got to the table, he was sure that she had made her Okra Surprise just out of meanness; he couldn't think of anything worse to serve to a guest. Aunt Wanda never took much to guests anyway, and the first thing she said after Earl Moller asked the blessing was, "I was sure I had nine quarts of applesauce left in the cellar, and now there's only eight."

"I guess you just miscounted," Mother said, passing the pork chops to Sam.

"Edna, I counted those jars and there were *nine!*" Aunt Wanda said again. "*Somebody's* been taking my applesauce."

Andy's heart began to thump. He could picture the worms upstairs in the applesauce and his stomach lurched.

Earl Moller was trying hard not to laugh. "Well, Wanda, you figure there's an applesauce thief on the loose? Somebody go to all the bother of breaking into this house just to make off with a quart of homemade applesauce? No offense to the applesauce, now."

"It dis*turbs* me, that's what!" Aunt Wanda said, and Andy began to wonder if she suspected him and Sam. "When I expect to find nine jars on the shelf, I don't want to find eight. Have some okra," she huffed, and pushed the dish toward Andy's friend.

Andy swallowed. To his amazement, however, Sam picked up the spoon and helped himself to a serving of okra. And then, as if that wasn't enough, he took another spoonful, and then a third. Andy stared. Sam picked up his knife and fork, cut the slimy green pods into pieces, and swallowed them.

From that moment on, Aunt Wanda couldn't stop smiling. Every time Andy looked over, Aunt Wanda was offering Sam another spoonful of peas, some strawberry jam, more mashed potatoes . . .

"I hear your mother makes some mighty fine biscuits," she told him.

Sam shook his head. "Nope, it's my dad. He does most of the cooking."

Now Aunt Wanda *really* stared. Mother, too.

"Did you bring the recipe?" Mother asked.

"Oh, yeah." Sam reached in the back pocket of his jeans and pulled out an index card he'd been sitting on all day at school. He handed it across the table to Aunt Wanda.

"Southern Split Biscuits," she read aloud, and Mother leaned over to see. "Look here, Edna, they've got mashed potatoes in them!"

"And look at all that butter and cream!" Mother said. "Oh, Wanda, we've got to try them out!"

Sam helped with the milking that evening. He wasn't much interested in shoveling out the muck in the stalls, but he wanted to know how the milking machine worked and Earl let him fasten the suction cups onto the cows.

"I'd like to come back sometime, bring my cousin," Sam said.

"You come back anytime you like," Earl told him. "Come in the summer, too, when we're haying. I can use a lot of help then."

By nine o'clock, the Mollers began going to bed.

Sam looked at Andy in dismay. "Evening's only getting started!" he said.

"Well, I've got to get up early," Andy told him. "I help Dad with the milking in the mornings."

"How early?" Sam asked, as they went upstairs.

"Five-thirty."

"Man, that's the middle of the night!"

Andy laughed. "Not for us it's not. You can sleep in if you want to."

The upper floor of the Mollers' house, where the eaves came down low, had one big room at the back where Wayne and Wendell slept, and two smaller rooms in front. Lois had one room and Andy the other. A big double bed took up most of Andy's room, and after he closed the door, Andy pulled out the wash basin to see how the worms were doing. Sam crouched down to look. The worms had made little wiggly lines in the applesauce.

"I've got another batch of worms in the freezer," Andy explained. "We'll take those tomorrow, since they're already dead. We can put both our lunches in your lunch pail, and the worms in mine. Then when we get to your place, we'll cook them."

"How much more you got to do before you write that essay?" Sam asked, getting into bed.

"I don't know." Andy sighed, crawling in beside him. "I should have at least three good recipes in it, though, or it won't be very good." He pulled the light cord and the room suddenly was dark. The boys watched the beam of moonlight that streamed in through the window.

"You figure if you were starving to death you could eat those worms?" Andy asked Sam.

"No," Sam told him. "Not unless I was delirious and didn't know what I was doing."

"Me neither."

"Wouldn't matter how dead they were, I'd still feel them crawling around in my stomach," Sam went on. "You know how if you cut a worm in half it makes two worms and they keep moving?"

"Yeah," said Andy, beginning to feel queasy.

"You figure beetles do the same? You figure all those little cut-up pieces of beetle you put in those brownies are going to turn into stomach beetles or something, like tapeworms?"

Andy felt his jaws tighten.

"Let's not talk anymore about it," he said, and pressed his lips together.

Andy was used to falling asleep almost as soon as he lay down. He could remember only a few times in his life when he had lain awake for any length of time. He was starting to nod off already when Sam said, "Sure is quiet around here. In town at least there are cars going by."

"Ummmph," said Andy, turning over.

"It's so quiet here you can hear the noises in your own head," said Sam.

Andy didn't answer. Little bits of dreams seemed to be drifting in and out of his mind. Then he felt Sam poke him.

"I hear 'em," Sam said.

Andy opened one eye. "Hear what?"

"Worms talking."

Andy smiled. "What are they saying?"

"They say they're so full of applesauce they're going to squirt the first person takes a bite of 'em."

Both boys began laughing then, and the next thing they knew, it was morning.

12

Better Than Colonel Sanders

ANDY DIDN'T HAVE TO RIDE THE BUS TO GET TO SAM'S after school. The two boys walked out the door of Bucksville Elementary, went down the sidewalk to Main Street, turned again, passed the Bucksville National Bank, the five-and-dime, the library, and Owens Hardware, and continued on to the Soul Food Kitchen and Carry-Out at the corner of Main and North Streets.

"Hey, Dad!" Sam said as he opened the door and a bell jangled.

"Hey, Sam!" said his father, who was cutting up fryers for supper. "How you doin', Andy?"

"Okay," Andy told him.

There was a rose-flowered curtain over the doorway at the back of the restaurant, and when Andy followed

Sam through it, he found himself in the Hollins' living room. A TV set was going in one corner and Sam's three-year-old sister, Denise, sat on a cushion in front of it watching "Sesame Street." There was a picture of Clay, Sam's older brother, on the wall.

"Home, Mom," Sam yelled to his mother.

"You bring Andy?"

"Yeah."

"How you doing, Andy?" Mrs. Hollins called from another room.

"Okay," Andy said again.

He sat down on the couch while Sam went off to get some Cokes. Denise shyly pulled her arms up on either side of her head and hid her face. Andy just smiled and watched the program with her. Bert and Ernie were arguing over a sandwich.

Andy thought about how, here in the Hollins' house and restaurant, it didn't make much difference what the weather was doing outside. It could be raining, snowing, dry or windy, and there could be hailstones big as golf balls falling on the sidewalk. Everything that really mattered was here inside these four walls. The only thing they had to worry about was that the customers kept coming. Weather was only a small concern.

At Andy's house, the weather forecast was the most important part of the day. That and the market report at noon. Andy wondered what it would be like to live all closed in like this. Sort of nice, he thought. Snug. Dad always seemed to have a problem on his mind. Should he sell the corn or buy feeder pigs, for example. No matter what he did, he always had to ask himself, "Will it pay?"

Sam came back in with two Cokes.

"Running a restaurant must be nice," Andy said. "You don't have to worry too much."

"You kidding me?" said Sam.

"What do you have to worry about?"

Sam leaned back against the sofa and took a long drink of his Coke, swallowing several times, then rested the bottle on his knee. "About whether another restaurant's going to open too close by and drive us out of business. About what if we charge too much and the customers go somewhere else. About whether the food we ordered is really fresh. . . . Worry's what we do best."

They sat watching "Sesame Street" with Denise until the Cookie Monster had made his appearance, and then Andy said, "When's the best time to cook them, when your dad won't notice?"

Sam sighed, as though, for a while, anyway, he'd forgotten the worms. "Wait till some customers come in and order chicken. Then I'll drop them in the fryer. You got them cut up?"

Andy nodded.

"My mom would die . . . ," Sam said.

About five-fifteen, the bell on the restaurant door chimed, meaning customers, and Sam went in to help his dad. This time Denise got up from her cushion in front of the TV and climbed on the couch beside Andy. She was wearing a bunny T-shirt and three different colored ribbons in her hair. Andy pointed to the bunny.

"Bear," he said.

Denise stared down at her T-shirt. She frowned and shook her head.

Andy grinned. "Gorilla," he said, pointing to her shirt again.

"*Bunny!*" Denise scolded.

A hand poked in through the curtain. "Okay," Sam whispered. "Give me the worms."

Quickly Andy opened his lunch bucket and took out a small plastic bag. The worms had thawed during the day and felt squishy inside the bag.

"Yuk," came Sam's voice when he felt them in the palm of his hand, and the hand disappeared again.

Mrs. Hollins came into the room with a stack of clean tablecloths that she had just finished ironing.

"Hope you like ham, Andy," she said, "because that's what we're having for dinner."

"I like it fine," Andy told her.

"You just make yourself at home now. We're not too busy on Tuesday evenings, so Sam should be through shortly." She put on a yellow apron and took the tablecloths into the restaurant.

Five minutes later, Sam dived through the curtained doorway, his cupped hands holding a few of the fried worms. They were coated with cornmeal and seasonings,

and looked like tiny pieces of chicken that had fallen off
during the frying.

"The rest are out there draining on a paper towel,"
Sam said. "I don't think Dad even noticed." He set them
on top of a newspaper on the coffee table and the boys
poked at them curiously.

"You get the feeling that any minute they're going to
crawl?" Sam said.

The door chimes tinkled again and Sam started
through the curtain once more. Suddenly he froze and
backed up.

"What's the matter?" Andy asked. "Who is it?"

"The inspector," breathed Sam.

"What inspector?"

"The health inspector. Comes by to check out the
restaurant every month or so."

"So?" said Andy. "The place looked fine to me."

"Those worms are sitting right there beside the fried
chicken," said Sam, and he looked ill.

Now it was Andy's turn to feel sick. He got up and
peeked through the curtain too. A woman was walking
slowly along the row of tables holding a clipboard. Every
now and then she ran her hand over a table top, or moved
a chair and peered down under a table. What if she discovered the worms? What if she reported it and Mr. Hollins
lost his license? In the space of thirty seconds, Andy imagined the Soul Food Kitchen and Carry-Out closing its
doors, the Hollins family going back to St. Louis, and

Aunt Wanda taking over. All because of him.

"I've got to get rid of those worms," Sam said, and moved on through the doorway. Andy stood back behind the curtain watching. The inspector had picked up an empty water glass and was holding it up to the light. She was getting closer and closer to the deep fat fryer where Sam's father was cooking more chicken. On a paper towel there on the counter sat a wing and thigh, cooling, and just to the right of them, scattered around the paper towel, were the rest of the fried worms. Sam started to move toward the fryer, but just then the inspector walked in front of him and went right over to where Mr. Hollins was standing.

"Ummm," she said, sniffing the air. "Certainly smells good in here."

Mr. Hollins smiled. "Special Spices," he told her. "Five more than Colonel Sanders uses on *his* chicken."

The inspector smiled too. "Garlic," she guessed, "ginger, pepper, paprika . . ." She reached out, and while Sam and Andy stared in horror, picked up one of the tiny pieces of fried worm and popped it in her mouth. Sam closed his eyes. Andy couldn't. He wished that he could . . . that he could just float away, but he couldn't even move.

"Chewy," the inspector was saying. "Tastes like . . . I don't see how it can, but it does . . . tastes like applesauce."

"Applesauce?" said Mr. Hollins.

"The secret ingredient," the inspector said. "Must be garlic, ginger, pepper, paprika, and applesauce." And she went over to inspect the shelves.

Sam came back through the curtain and the boys sank down on the couch, too weak to say a word. Too late, they discovered that while their backs were turned, Denise had eaten all the fried worms on the coffee table.

"More!" Denise said, licking her fingers.

"Mom would die . . . !" Sam said again.

They rescued the rest of the worms as soon as the inspector left, and dropped them in the garbage. If Denise and the health inspector thought they were delicious, that was good enough for Andy's essay. Andy didn't want to see another fried worm in his life; didn't even want to think about it.

Suppertime at the Hollins' was a lot later than it was at the Mollers'. On the farm, suppertime was five-thirty or six, just before Earl Moller went out to milk the cows. But here at the Soul Food Kitchen, the Hollins waited until most of the customers had gone before they set up the table for themselves near the back. Sam's parents were in a good mood because the health inspector had given them a high rating.

There were biscuits with the ham, and mashed turnips and spinach, and nobody said anything when Andy let the spinach go by without taking any. But he wished that he *had* taken some. Wished that he *could*. That he could just open his mouth the way Sam had done at the

Mollers' table and swallow the dinner down. Spinach was like having a mouth full of seaweed, though. It was like swallowing and feeling a string go halfway down your throat.

Mrs. Hollins was still talking about the inspector.

"I wonder why she thought the chicken tasted like applesauce?" she asked her husband.

He shook his head. "Only took a nibble—a bit of the skin, I imagine—but she sure thought it was good."

Andy didn't dare lift his eyes to look at Sam, but they kicked each other under the table.

Travers came over after dinner. His father owned the barbershop down the street, and the three boys played Parcheesi till bedtime, then Travers went home.

It was strange sleeping in Sam's room. Sam slept in a single bed, and there was a trundlebed for Andy, that pulled out from underneath so that they were sleeping on two different levels. When a car drove by outside it seemed to Andy as though it were coming right through the window. The car lights shone on the ceiling and moved on across the wall.

"Sam?" Andy said finally, wondering if his friend was awake.

"Yeah?"

"Do you and Travers always get along?"

"Most of the time we do."

"How?"

"What do you mean, 'how'? He's the only cousin I've

got—in Iowa, anyway. Didn't come all the way up here from St. Louis just to fight with him."

Andy thought that over. Jack was *his* only cousin in Iowa, too, but it didn't seem to matter. It seemed to make it worse—as though the fact that Aunt Bernie had bragged so much about Jack when he was little was going to go on making the boys enemies for the rest of their lives. Andy sighed and rolled over.

"Sam?" he said again.

"Yeah?"

"How did you eat that okra?"

The bed squeaked and Sam sat up on one elbow. "What?"

"That okra at my house. Aunt Wanda's Okra Surprise. How'd you get it down?"

"What are you talking about? I just put it in my mouth and swallowed."

"But it's stringy! It's slimy! It feels like seaweed!" Andy protested.

"You're talking about how it feels, I'm talking how it *tastes,*" said Sam. "That's what we put in gumbo, and it tastes good."

Long after Sam had fallen asleep, Andy lay there thinking about okra. Maybe he *hadn't* thought enough about how things tasted—only how they looked and how they felt and how the names sounded. Okra tasted good? Maybe sometime, like in a hundred years or so, he might take a nibble and find out.

13

~~~~~~~~~~~~~~~~~~~~~~~~~~~~~~~~~~~~~~

Getting Even

ANDY FELT THAT HE NEEDED AT LEAST ONE MORE thing to cook for his essay. Grasshoppers wouldn't be around for another month, crickets till July. He looked up larvae and pupae in the encyclopedia, and decided to get some ant pupae to mix with egg salad.

"Sorry to bother you guys," he said to the ants that swarmed out of the ant hill he'd found by the barn, "but I need some pupae, whatever the heck they are." The very word sounded awful, and Andy was glad he didn't have to eat them himself.

When you disturb an anthill, the encyclopedia had said, *the little white bundles that the worker ants may be seen carrying away in their jaws are not ant eggs, as some people think, but larvae or pupae.* Andy was relieved they weren't ant eggs. He didn't particularly mind taking a few ant teenagers, if that's what pupae were, but he sure didn't want to take the babies.

He only got three pupae from that nest and had a time getting even those away from the worker ants. After nineteen anthills, he only had enough pupae to fill a teaspoon. The problem with serving insects for dinner, Andy discovered, was that you had to have a lot of them. Still, if somebody had more time than money, he could stretch his groceries with a good hearty meal of earthworms now and then.

Andy decided at last to look for mealworm grubs that the man from the University had said could be found where grain was stored. Andy remembered seeing them once when he and his father replaced one of the boards near the haymow. He took a screwdriver and poked around between the boards near the hay and, sure enough, he found those fat whitish inch-long grubs that were pictured in the encyclopedia. When he had finally gathered a few tablespoons of them, he decided that was enough to mix with egg salad for Lois's sandwich at the game that afternoon. He didn't have to make the whole sandwich out of grubs.

Egg salad just happened to be Lois' favorite sandwich, and one of the few things that Andy could make himself: Two chopped hard-boiled eggs, one stalk of chopped celery, a little onion salt, parsley, and pepper mixed together with mayonnaise and mustard. This time, however, when Andy boiled the eggs, he dropped the pupae in the water too, and when they had boiled for a minute or so, he took them out, cooled them, chopped them, and mixed them with the eggs after they were done. There was enough for two sandwiches. Andy left one in the refrigerator and packed the other for the ball game, along with the bats and gloves.

The *Bucksville Beagles* were playing the *Hawkeye Hounds* down by the Ruby Theater. Mother and Aunt Wanda climbed in the front seat of the station wagon and Andy and Lois got in back. Every time they passed another car on the road, Lois would stick her head out the window and bellow, "Yeah, *Beagles! Bucksville Beagles!*"

"She should have been born a boy, Edna," Aunt Wanda said once. "Wayne, Wendell, and Andy all three don't make as much noise as that girl."

This time Sam and Travers had walked over to watch the game and were sitting up in the top row of bleachers. The bleachers were full of *Hawkeye* fans too, and there was scarcely room enough for Jack and Aunt Bernadine, when they arrived, to squeeze into the second row behind Andy.

The game began, and Shirley, the *Beagles'* pitcher, had a whole row of fans. No matter what she did, the junior-high boys thought she was wonderful. If the umpire called Shirley for delaying the game, a boy said that he was crazy. If the umpire said the ball didn't cross home plate, a boy was on his feet protesting. When the *Beagles* came off the field to bat, boys called out things like, "Hey, Shirley, I'm batty about you!" and "Hey, Beautiful, I sure do like your swing!" Mother and Aunt Wanda rolled their eyes. Andy wondered if he would ever act like that when he got to be thirteen. Even Jack was yelling and acting crazy.

Jack yelled so much, in fact, that his throat got dry, and he kept helping himself to water from the jug.

"That's for the *team,* Jack," Andy told him.

"*I'm* on the team," Jack would say. "I'm the cheering section." Aunt Bernie didn't even stop him.

At the end of the fourth inning, however, the *Hounds* were ahead by seven. Lois came over and slumped beside Andy, her head down, elbows resting on her knees. The *Beagles* were striking out one after another. Andy felt sorry for his sister. He wanted to offer her the sandwich he'd made, but when he remembered what was in it, he had second thoughts.

"Got my sandwich?" Lois asked glumly.

Andy swallowed. "Yeah," he said, and handed it to her.

Lois unwrapped it without even looking, then sat holding it in her hands, staring out at the field where the game was going from bad to worse.

"That egg salad?" said Jack, leaning over Andy's shoulder. "Hey, I *love* egg salad!"

"That's for Lois," Andy told him.

"Half's for Lois, half's for me," Jack said, snatching a section of it from her hand.

"Jack!" yelled Andy, turning around.

But Lois just shrugged and handed Jack the other half as well. "You can have it," she said, as the third batter struck out. "I'm not hungry anyway." And she walked back out on the field.

It was as though it were meant to be, Andy decided. This was even better than the brownies. He listened as Jack smacked his lips and took a big bite.

That's for the time you took me out in the corn and left me, Andy thought as Jack chewed. Jack swallowed and took another bite.

That's for taking me to the mailbox when the turkey was loose, Andy thought.

Two more bites. Chomp. Chomp. *That's for the day you chased me around the yard on your bicycle and the day you locked me in the barn,* Andy breathed silently.

He didn't know when he had felt so good. Even as his stomach churned at the idea of mealworm grubs in egg salad, he pictured himself turning to Jack and saying, "Hey, Jack, guess what you just ate?" He couldn't, of course, but he couldn't help smiling, either. This was the third recipe that had turned out all right. Now he could write his essay and hand it in.

The *Beagles* lost and Lois didn't even want to join the team at the Dairy Queen. She just wanted to go home. But she never stayed upset for long. By the time Andy had put the equipment away in the bat box in the barn, he found Lois standing by the kitchen table, drinking a glass of milk and eating the second sandwich.

14

Okra Surprise

WHEN THE DEADLINE ARRIVED ON MAY 25, NINE STU-
dents handed in essays for the contest.

Andy had spent the weekend writing his on scratch
paper and then, when he had checked all the spelling,
wrote it out carefully once again on good white paper:
"How Beetles, Bugs, and Worms Can Save Money and the
Food Supply Both," he had titled it.

He told how larvae and pupae could be good sources
of fat and protein, how to prepare the worms and beetles,
and he offered three recipes for cooking them: beetles,
lightly toasted, could be used as nuts in brownies; earthworms, rolled in seasoned cornmeal, could be deep-fried
in place of chicken; and larvae, simmered gently, could be
used in egg salad. He gave his own recipe for egg salad.

"Since you can get earthworms and beetles from the same land that you grow corn on," Andy wrote, "you don't have to have any more space to harvest insects. You just use the land you've got." He said that if a family worked hard, they could save 25 percent of the money they usually spent on meat. Andy wasn't sure of that figure, but it seemed reasonable enough to him.

It was a wonderful feeling to have the essay done. Not only that, but in ten days the winner would be announced and in just twelve days, school would be out. In the meantime, there was the Annual Memorial Day Parade to look forward to.

The Memorial Day Parade was about the biggest event in Bucksville, because there was a lot of memorializing to do. Anybody who had ever died was to be remembered, of course, and especially anybody who had died in a war. In addition, all the brave pioneer women who had given their lives helping to settle the land west of the Mississippi River were to be remembered, and there was a statue in the middle of Bucksville of a woman wearing a sunbonnet and carrying a rifle, just to make sure you didn't forget. Also to be remembered was Luther Sudermann's great-grandfather, who had started the first newspaper in Bucksville, and Horace Buck, for whom Bucksville was named. There was even a bronze plaque in the sidewalk outside Prescott's Drugstore remembering Buck, because it was said that on that very spot, before there were sidewalks, of course, he had been killed by a Sioux

Indian. The arrow had been preserved for a time in the county museum until an expert on Indian culture examined it and said it wasn't an Indian arrow at all. But the plaque remained in the sidewalk nonetheless.

On the day of the parade Lois left for town early, because she was marching with the junior-high school cheerleaders, and Wayne and Wendell were riding on the Future Farmers of America float. Andy wasn't thrilled to have to sit in the back seat of the station wagon beside Aunt Wanda and the picnic basket, but the wonderful smells of baked beans, brown sugar cake, blueberry cobbler, and potato salad kept his mind on the meal to come. When it wasn't on what he had done to Aunt Wanda's Okra Surprise, that is.

He wasn't quite sure why he had done it, because he didn't need any more recipes. But that morning, just after Aunt Wanda had taken her Okra Surprise casserole out of the oven and gone to change her dress, Andy had taken three of his frozen earthworms, chopped them up fine, and mixed them carefully in with the bubbling green pods in the baking dish. The okra seemed to hiss and spit at him as he stirred. He had intended, actually, to put all his remaining earthworms in the okra, but felt that might be overdoing it a bit. Aunt Wanda had come back into the kitchen, wrapped the casserole in several layers of newspaper to keep it hot during the parade, and set off with the Mollers for town.

Mother and Aunt Wanda placed their folding chairs

in front of the hardware store, where you could not only see the parade as it passed, but watch it turn the corner at Union Street too. Andy never sat on a folding chair at a parade if he could help it. If you got there early enough, you could ask your dad to boost you up on the wide window ledge just above the door of Owens Hardware. This year, there was just space enough beside Sam and Travers and Russ for Andy to squeeze in too. Jack, down below, had to sit with his mother. Andy smiled to himself.

He could see where the parade was gathering far down Main Street near Farley's Feed Store. Finally he heard the distant sound of the drum, then the horns, and the parade began to move.

The majorette came first, leading the Bucksville High School Band. The cheerleaders from Bucksville Junior High came next waving their green pompons, then the 4-H Club float with a big chocolate cake in the middle made of styrofoam. Miss Fayette County followed in a spangled dress and jacket, riding in the back of a pickup, followed by a huge 280-horsepower tractor with eight wheels and an air-conditioned cab, advertising the Farmers' Co-op. Behind the tractor was an old Chevy convertible with Bucksville's oldest resident, Mrs. Emma Grant, age ninety-one, holding Bucksville's youngest resident, the two-and-a-half-week-old daughter of the high-school wrestling coach. There were the Gospel Light Singers from the Faith and Hope Church of the Savior, the Fayette County Hog and Trade Show float, a special contingent of the

Veterans of Foreign Wars, and bringing up the rear was a car advertising the Lutheran Assistance League.

The one thing about watching a parade in Bucksville, Andy thought, was that you knew almost everyone in it. You might never get your picture in the county paper, but if you lived to be at least thirty, you'd have marched in a parade at some time or other. The only reason everybody wasn't in it was because there had to be someone left to do the watching.

When the Lutheran Assistance League car had finally turned the corner at Union Street and the small children who had been fidgeting about on the sidewalk swarmed out into the street to prance after it, the women all crossed over to the park to spread their food out on the long picnic tables.

The wonderful thing about a town picnic was that the food seemed to stretch for miles and you could go back for more as often as you liked. Even after the speeches began in the bandstand and the adults sat listening, children could go back to the tables and help themselves to six or seven cookies or a third piece of cake, and nobody blinked an eye. When the band finally reappeared from the opposite direction, people began lining up with plastic plates and spoons at each of the long tables. When their plates were filled, they sat down wherever they could find a spot.

Andy heaped his plate high with macaroni and cheese, fried chicken, country ham, baked beans, pineapple salad, brown sugar cake, and a cup of Kool Aid. He sat down on the steps of the library with his father, Aunt Bernadine, Aunt Wanda, and Jack.

Nobody said anything for the first few minutes, because the parade had gone on so long and everyone was hungry. The food tasted too good to ruin it by talking.

After a while, however, when they slowed down, Aunt Bernie said, "You won't guess what we had for dinner last night, Earl. Fillet of flounder cooked in the dishwasher. It was Jack's idea, and I want to tell you it was delicious."

Andy stared.

"The *dish* washer!" said Aunt Wanda.

Jack was beaming like he'd won the Kentucky Derby.

"What's the point?" asked Andy's father.

"It's his essay for the Roger B. Sudermann Contest. Tell them, Jack."

Jack took another bite of his roll and talked with his mouth half full. "Well," he said, "I wrote about conserving energy. I was trying to figure out how a woman could cook while she was doing something else. If she saved the breakfast dishes, see, and did them just before supper, she could steam the fish while she did the dishes."

"Merciful heavens, wouldn't it taste like Cascade?" asked Aunt Wanda.

"Well, it did the first time. The second time we just ran the dishwasher without the dishes and the detergent," Jack said. "I mean, it was just an experiment."

Andy was so envious he could hardly stand it. Now

all the other things Jack had done began to make sense. A woman could buy hamburger at the store and have it frying on the engine of her car while she drove home (if she didn't set fire to the car, of course). If her child was sick with a cold, she could make hot chocolate for him while she ran the vaporizer. If she was doing the ironing and was too busy to stop for lunch, she could make herself a grilled cheese sandwich there at the ironing board. Jack was a real brain, all right.

"What was your essay about, Andy?" Aunt Bernie asked.

"Oh, nothing much," Andy said, busily separating his fried chicken from the pineapple salad and the baked beans from the ham and the macaroni from the brown sugar cake. Compared to Jack's, his essay didn't sound so great.

Aunt Bernie started to ask him something else, but just then Aunt Wanda stopped eating and said, "I don't know what it is, but my okra tastes different."

"Tastes okay to me," said Andy's father.

"Well, it's *different!*" Aunt Wanda said again. "Bernadine, you taste it."

Andy sat without moving as Aunt Bernie reached across him to jab her fork into Aunt Wanda's helping of Okra Surprise. The fork went back in Aunt Bernie's mouth and her jaws moved up and down.

"Hmmm," said Jack's mother.

"It's *different,* isn't it?" said Aunt Wanda.

"Tastes like applesauce," said Aunt Bernie.

"Applesauce!" cried Aunt Wanda. "I didn't get apples anywhere *near* that okra!"

And suddenly Andy realized that not only could he not answer any questions just then about his essay, but he didn't know when he could tell anyone at all. If he told them about the worms and beetles, they would want to know how he had fixed them, and if he told them how he'd fixed them, they'd want to know if he'd eaten any. One thing would lead to another, and Aunt Wanda would find out what he had done to her Okra Surprise. And now, as desperately as Andy had once hoped he would win the contest, he began to hope that he wouldn't.

15

Who Won the Contest

ON JUNE 4, TWO DAYS BEFORE SCHOOL WAS OUT, MRS. Haynes' class sat waiting as Luther Sudermann's car pulled up outside the window. As they watched him shake hands with the principal, the teacher said, "No matter who wins the contest, I want you to know that I read all the essays myself before I sent them to Mr. Sudermann, and I think that every one of them was good. *All* of you who entered the contest deserve to feel proud of what you've done."

There were footsteps in the hall, then the principal came in, followed by a gray-haired man in a blue suit. His eyes seemed to take in the whole room at once, and he smiled as the principal introduced him. Then he sat down on the edge of Mrs. Haynes' desk and looked the students over.

"I was disappointed," he said, "that only nine of you decided to enter my contest this year, but I'm delighted with those who did. It just goes to show that imagination is alive and well in these United States, and if the future of our country depends on people like you, then we're in good hands."

The principal beamed.

Mr. Sudermann went on to talk about his son Roger when he was alive, and how Roger was always building something or taking it apart.

"If something broke around the house, Roger would say, 'Maybe I can fix it, Dad,' and when he saw something new, he'd say, 'Show me how it works.' He was intellectually curious—always tried to improve things, make them a little better." Mr. Sudermann bowed his head for a moment and stared at the floor. "Needless to say, I miss him," he told the class, "but through this contest, I can keep the idea of him alive—I can keep his imagination going, and reward others who show the same inventiveness as Roger."

Andy had never known anything about Roger Sudermann before, and could almost see the boy that Mr. Sudermann was talking about. He was wondering, too, if *he* ever died young, what his dad would say about *him*. That Andy was imaginative? Helpful? Open to new ideas?

"To the nine of you who entered my contest," Mr. Sudermann went on, "I want you to know that I have read your essays carefully—some of them several times. I narrowed my choice down to five, then four, then three, and I had a very hard time narrowing it down to two. But once I had eliminated all but two, I simply could go no further, and so—for the first time in the history of the Roger B. Sudermann contest—I am declaring two winners this year, and each will receive a check for fifty dollars. The two winning essays were: "Saving Energy When You Cook," by Jack Barth, and "How Beetles, Bugs, and Worms Can Save Money and the Food Supply Both," by Andy Moller. Would you two boys come up here, please?"

The class began to clap as Andy, swallowing, stood up and moved numbly to the front of the classroom beside Jack. The teacher and principal were clapping too.

Mr. Sudermann shook both boys' hands. "I saw a little of my son in what each of you boys wrote," he said, "and I know that if Roger were alive, he'd want to be your friend. You have both shown the spirit of initiative and creativity that Mrs. Sudermann and I so admire, and on June 10, I am going to feel very honored to shake your hands again on the steps of the library."

"Thank you," said Jack.

"Thank you," said Andy, barely audible.

The principal walked Mr. Sudermann back out to his car again, and Mrs. Haynes beamed at Jack and Andy.

"Read their essays out loud!" someone said.

"Yes!" said the others.

"Isn't it lucky that I made copies?" Mrs. Haynes

smiled, and took them out of her drawer. Andy stared down at his feet.

Mrs. Haynes read Jack's essay first. Everybody laughed when she read the part about the hamburgers almost catching fire under the hood of the car. The class clapped when the essay was over, and Mrs. Haynes said she was looking forward to cooking fish in her dishwasher. Then she picked up Andy's essay.

When it was clear that Andy was talking about *eating* beetles, bugs, and worms, there were gasps.

"Oh, gross!" someone giggled.

"Eeeyuuk!" said somebody else.

Andy saw Sam look over at him nervously and smile. He tried to smile back but his face felt frozen. When Mrs. Haynes read about using little bits of beetles, lightly toasted, in brownies, the room suddenly got very quiet. And when at last she finished reading, nobody clapped. Sam started to, then stopped. Mrs. Haynes looked around, puzzled.

"Wasn't that a good essay, class?" she said. "I suppose it might take some getting used to, but there is really no reason why we can't use insects as a source of protein."

Dora Kray raised her hand. "What if somebody gives you a brownie with beetles in it and doesn't tell you?"

The teacher thought about it. "Well, I think everyone has the right, certainly, to know what he's eating, but . . ." She looked around, puzzled. "Andy wouldn't do . . ." She stopped.

The room was embarrassingly quiet, and Mrs. Haynes didn't quite know what to do. Finally she asked everyone to take out his arithmetic book, and she started the morning's lesson.

"Listen, they had to find out sooner or later," Sam said to Andy at recess when the others walked by without talking to him. "Heck, they'll get over it. They'll forget."

"Go on and play kickball with them," Andy said. "I don't want them mad at you, too."

It was one of the most horrible days Andy had ever spent. Whenever the other students walked by his desk, they either looked the other way or glared at him. Jack, strangely, spoke to him on the bus going home, but no one else did. Andy didn't know just how he was going to tell his family. He was relieved, when he reached the house, that Mother had forgotten what day it was, and she and Aunt Wanda were busily putting up pints of strawberry jam.

In a matter of minutes, however, the phone rang and it was Aunt Bernie, telling Mother that both Jack and Andy had won the contest together, and Mother said she would call her back later, that the preserves were boiling.

"For heaven's sake, Andy, you didn't even tell us," Mother said, turning back to the stove. "How wonderful!"

Andy faked a smile.

"You're going to have to tell us all about it at supper," she went on. "Won't your dad be pleased, though?"

"What did you write about?" Aunt Wanda asked,

pouring a pitcherful of sugar into the pot of boiling berries.

"Oh, saving money on groceries," Andy said.

"Well, I'll be glad to hear how to do that!" Mother told him.

Andy went out in the barn and began shoveling out the stalls. The whole fifth-grade class was mad at him, and he couldn't much blame them. In another hour or so, the entire family would be angry, too. He didn't see how saying that he was sorry would help. What was done was done, and no one would ever forget it.

At supper that evening, Dad had no sooner asked the blessing than Mother said, "Andy has some good news tonight. Tell them, Andy."

Andy swallowed. His cheeks felt as though they would crack if he tried to make them smile once more. "I was one of the winners of the Roger B. Sudermann Contest," he said. "There were two winners this year, and Jack was the other one."

"Isn't that marvelous?" said Mother. "Did Mr. Sudermann come to school and announce the winners himself?"

Andy told them about the little speech Mr. Sudermann had given the class, glad to turn the attention away from himself. He said how Luther Sudermann had told them that Roger was always inventing things, trying to find out how something worked.

"He *was* the boy who came to school as a TV set!" Lois said suddenly. "I remember now! He was wearing this box with knobs, and his face was where the screen would be. When you turned one knob, he gave you a dog food commercial, and when you turned the other one, he shut up."

"Well!" said Andy's father. "We'll have to read that essay you wrote. What was it about?"

"Saving money on groceries," said Aunt Wanda. "I'd certainly like to know how Andy knows anything about that."

"What did you call your essay?" Wendell asked, reaching for another slice of beef.

Andy took a deep breath and put down his fork. "How Beetles, Bugs, and Worms Can Save Money and the Food Supply Both,' " he said.

The family stared at him.

"How can they do *that?*" asked Mother.

Andy's face felt flushed. His tongue seemed to be swelling. "You eat them," he said.

"*Eat* them?" cried Lois.

Andy continued staring down at his hands. "I wrote to a man at the University and he told me how to fix them."

"*Safely?*" said Mother.

Andy nodded.

"Did you *try* it?" she asked.

"I cooked them," Andy said, not quite answering.

Suddenly no one was eating.

"What . . . did . . . you . . . cook?" came Aunt Wanda's voice, slow and steady.

Andy closed his eyes. "Brownies . . . ," he said.

He heard Wendell cough.

"Deep-fried worms . . ."

The family seemed to have stopped breathing.

"And . . . grubs in egg salad."

"Egg salad!" Lois leaped up, tipping over her chair. "Not *my* egg salad!"

Andy didn't answer.

A long, piercing shriek filled the kitchen, rattling the walls. "Arrrrgggggh!" Lois lunged for the sink, stuck her mouth under the faucet and turned the water on full force. "Yauuugghh!" she screamed again, gargling and screeching, both at the same time.

"Andy," said Aunt Wanda, and her voice was like lead weights. "Did you touch my Okra Surprise?"

Andy couldn't answer that either, and continued staring down at his lap. And at that very moment, the phone rang.

16

Beetles, Lightly Toasted

ANDY GOT UP FROM THE TABLE AND ANSWERED THE phone because he needed an excuse to leave. If he could have sailed out the window and over the treetops, he would have done so gladly. A ringing telephone was the next best thing. It saved him from simply getting up from the table and going upstairs to his room, which was what he was about to do anyway.

"Could I speak to Andy Moller, please?" said a man's voice at the other end.

"I'm Andy."

"Good! This is Frank Harris, a photographer from the *Bucksville Gazette.* Mr. Sudermann told me about you winning the essay contest—you and another boy—and we'd like to get a photo of the winners."

It was what Andy had been waiting for for two years —the reason he had entered the contest. Now, the last thing in the world he wanted was his picture in the *Bucksville Gazette,* but there was no way he could get out of it.

"You're the one who wrote about beetles and bugs, aren't you?" the photographer asked.

"Yes . . ."

"Well, what Mr. Sudermann has in mind, see, is a photo of you right there on the steps of the library eating one of those meals you wrote about."

Andy's arm went weak at the elbow and he almost dropped the receiver.

"You . . . you can't just take a picture of us standing on the steps?" he asked.

"Not much action in that. We're looking for a human-interest photo. Mr. Sudermann said he'll bring the chair and table on June 10, and you bring your lunch. Okay? We got ourselves a deal?"

It was like being asked to go over Niagara Falls in a barrel; to wade in a river with snakes. Eating a brownie without knowing there were beetles in it was bad enough, but sitting down to a meal of beetles, worms, and grubs, and *knowing* it was beyond anything he could imagine. The entire fifth-grade class was mad at him, however. He'd been a disappointment to Mrs. Haynes and his family too. Eating that meal himself was the only way that he could ever make up for what he'd done. He swallowed.

"Andy?" the photographer said.

Andy swallowed again. "Okay," he said. "I'll do it."

Then he hung up the phone and, with his family staring after him, went upstairs to his room.

No one but Jack spoke to him on the bus the next morning. Andy wondered why Jack bothered. He could have turned up his nose at Andy so easily, like everyone else was doing. Maybe, as Mother had said, Jack really *was* lonely, and knew how it felt.

At recess, however, Sam sat beside Andy on the steps, and Andy told him what the photographer had asked.

"Man, this sure turned out different than you thought," Sam said after they'd sat a while in silence. "What are you going to do?"

"I'm going to eat that lunch," Andy said.

Sam swallowed. "Maybe you just have to put your fork in it and *look* like you're eating," he suggested.

Andy shook his head. "That would be enough for the newspaper, but not for the people who were standing there watching."

Sam moaned as if in pain. "And you can't fake it," he said. "Just wouldn't be right. You've really got to put bugs in those brownies."

Andy nodded. He tried to think of what could be worse. If he had his choice of eating that lunch or breaking his leg, would he still rather break his leg? If someone told him he could walk down the street in his underpants or eat those beetles, would he still rather walk down the street in his underpants?

"It's all how you look at it," Sam said, still trying to help. "You know those dudes who walk over hot coals? You know how they sleep on nails? It's all up here," Sam said, tapping his forehead.

"So?" said Andy.

"So when it's time for you to eat those worms, you think applesauce—little tubes of applesauce—that's all you're eating. You get those beetles in your mouth, you think cornflakes."

"I'll try," said Andy.

That evening, as Andy helped his father with the milking, WMT played a song about a long-distance trucker who was running away from love, and then it was time for the eastern roundup—"News from our neighboring counties," the announcer said. Andy was only half listening as he rolled the big milk cans across the floor, but then the announcer said, ". . . and from Bucksville comes word that there are *two* winners this year in the annual Roger B. Sudermann Contest—one boy who cooks fish in the dishwasher and another who eats toasted beetles and worms. That's right, folks. In a contest rewarding ingenuity and imagination among fifth graders, these two boys propose to save energy and money by cooking in unusual ways and digging up food in the backyard." And here the announcer broke into a song: "Nobody loves me, everybody hates me, guess I'll go eat worms." Then he laughed and said, "These boys are serious, though, and on June 10, Jack Barth and Andy Moller each will receive an award

and a check from Luther Sudermann, publisher of the
Bucksville Gazette, who organized the contest in memory
of his son. Congratulations, boys, but just don't invite me
over for dinner, huh . . . ?"

Andy turned his back to the radio and sat down
weakly on a bale of hay.

"Well, Andy," said his father, "you got yourself into
this, and it wasn't such a bad idea—only the way you went
about it. How do you figure to set things right?"

"I'm going to eat that stuff myself," Andy told him.

His father was quiet for a moment as he moved to
another group of cows and attached the cups of the milking machine. "How d'you figure that's going to help?"

"I'm going to do it on the steps of the library," Andy
said. "A photographer's going to take a picture of it. It
was Mr. Sudermann's idea."

Andy couldn't quite tell if his father was laughing or
not. There was certainly a smile in his voice when he said,
"Well, I'll say this—it sure is going to make a lot of people
awful happy."

Dad must have told Mother and she must have told
Aunt Wanda, and after that, it was only a matter of time
before Lois, Wayne, and Wendell heard about it and the
whole of Bucksville besides. Lois, who had not spoken to
Andy since the night she gargled in the sink, treated him
more politely, cautiously, like a prisoner who was about
to be shot.

The night before the award ceremony, Andy

dreamed that he was eating spinach, only it was made of green worms—stringy worms—and he couldn't seem to swallow them; they just went halfway down his throat and then wouldn't go either way.

The next day Andy got up, did his chores in the barn, and went to the cellar for the last remaining frozen worms beneath his mother's pies. He set them on the kitchen counter along with the jar containing the last of the toasted beetle bits, then went out in the barn with a screwdriver to find a few more mealworm grubs between the floorboards. Mother had taken Lois into town early for a haircut, and they would meet Andy on the steps of the library at noon before they did the rest of their errands. Dad and Wayne and Wendell were cultivating and wouldn't be able to come, but at least they would see Andy's picture in the paper, they told him.

Back in the kitchen, Andy had just got out the flour and chocolate for the brownies when he heard a voice behind him saying, "Need any help, Andy?"

Aunt Wanda came in the kitchen and put on her apron.

At first he was going to say no, but he didn't know much about deep-frying in fat.

"Well," he said, "I can make the brownies and the egg salad, but I'm not sure how to . . . uh . . ."

"Fry worms," said Aunt Wanda.

"Yeah," said Andy. "Sam fried them before in his dad's restaurant—just dropped them in the batter when his dad was frying chicken—but I didn't want to ask him again. . . ."

"Last thing in the world a new restaurant needs is a rumor going around that it fries worms," said Aunt Wanda. "If I can deep-fry chicken, I can deep-fry worms. Let me have them."

By eleven-thirty the lunch was packed in a brown paper bag, Andy had on his good trousers and shirt, and sat in the front seat of Wendell's pickup with Aunt Wanda at the wheel. There had been an announcement in the paper that morning that Andy would be eating his "conservation lunch" on the steps of the public library at twelve noon, and it listed the menu, which the reporter had jazzed up a bit:

> Earthworms, en Brochette
> Grub on Seeded Roll
> Beetle Brownies

This is how it feels to go to war, Andy thought as they passed fields where corn was already ankle high and cows were munching contentedly in pastures. The clouds looked like swirls of whipped cream, and the breeze floating in the window carried the scent of clover. But it all seemed to be for someone else to enjoy, not Andy.

Aunt Wanda was surprisingly kind. Andy noticed that she had made his grub sandwich as attractive as possible, with a big piece of crisp lettuce and sesame roll.

But Andy knew that even if she had served the roll on a silver platter with caramel sauce over the top, it still wouldn't have disguised what was in it.

His heart began to thump harder as the pickup turned down Main Street. It looked as though the entire fifth-grade class was there, plus their parents and a dozen other people besides. Mother and Lois were standing off to one side, Mother looking concerned. There was a card table and a folding chair at the bottom of the library steps, and a photographer stood nearby, talking with Mr. Sudermann. People were looking out of the door of the bank and from the upper windows of Owens Hardware.

Jack was already there with Aunt Bernadine, and when Andy walked up the steps beside him, Jack whispered, in awe,

"Andy, you really going to do it?"

"Yes," said Andy.

Mr. Sudermann gave the same speech he had given in the classroom, but this time he said that it was four years ago exactly that Roger fell off the silo, and in memory of his son's inquisitiveness and ingenuity, he was happy to present two awards this year to boys who had proved that a mind is capable of better things than simply watching TV.

"Farmers, and sons and daughters of farmers, after all, know the value of land, and the importance of thrift and conservation of all our natural resources. And so, with conservation as the theme this year, it is with great pleasure that I present Jack Barth with the Roger B. Sudermann award and a check for fifty dollars for his ideas on conserving energy by cooking in unusual ways with alternate sources of heat."

He handed Jack a little bronze pin that said "Imagination," then a check from his vest pocket, and finally he shook his hand.

"Congratulations," he said.

"Thank you," said Jack. The people clapped and the photographer snapped a picture.

"And it is with equally great pleasure that I present Andy Moller with an award for his essay on unusual sources of food to provide fat and protein in the diet," Mr. Sudermann said. He gave Andy the other pin and the other check, then shook his hand also.

"Congratulations," he said.

"Thank you," said Andy, and again the people clapped and the photographer snapped his shutter.

Mr. Sudermann smiled down at Andy. "Well now, Andy, I believe you promised a demonstration of just how tasty your recipes can be."

The crowd smiled and pushed a little closer. Sam and Travers were there, and Sam looked worried. Russ Zumbach and Dora Kray were there in front too, grinning. They did not look worried. As Dad had said, this was going to make a lot of people very happy. Everyone was waiting for the main attraction.

Andy went to the card table and sat down. He took

his lunch from out of the bag and spread it out before him on the card table. There was a muffled giggle from Jack, who had gone back to stand beside Aunt Bernie.

Andy unwrapped the deep-fried worms and set them on top the brown bag. Then he unwrapped the grub sandwich with the Boston lettuce, and finally the chocolate brownie with the beetle backs glistening in the dough.

He tried to keep his jaw steady. *Tubes of applesauce,* Sam had said about the worms. The photographer was squatting down at eye level, tipping the camera. Jack giggled out loud this time, and Aunt Bernie poked him with her elbow.

Suddenly Andy looked up at Mr. Sudermann. "It doesn't seem right for me to enjoy this all by myself," he smiled. "Jack was a winner, too. He can share it with me."

Jack's face went gray.

"Good idea!" said Mr. Sudermann, and to the photographer, "Get both of them in the picture. That's better yet."

Jack tried to protest that he wasn't hungry, but Mr. Owens from the hardware store picked up one of his empty nail kegs from out front and passed it over. "There you go," he said.

Jack sat down weakly on the keg and stared at the lunch before him. Andy divided everything in half: The brownie, the sandwich, and the four fried worms, giving Jack, naturally—his guest—the larger share.

"Okay, now, *big* bite," the photographer was saying, holding the camera up to his eye.

Andy lifted the grub sandwich to his lips. *Just pretend,* he told himself, *that you can either fall off the silo or take a bite of this sandwich.*

The bread moved even closer. Nothing would ever be so hard to swallow again—not even Aunt Wanda's Okra Surprise, Andy knew.

Crunch. His teeth bit into the roll and then the lettuce. Little chewy lumps of something settled on his tongue. Struggling not to gag, Andy swallowed as soon as he could.

"Yuk!" somebody said in the crowd.

Jack was still staring at his half of the sandwich.

Andy took another bite. Crunch again. The roll was fresh, the lettuce was crisp, and then he remembered what Sam had told him—that it doesn't matter what a food is called, or how it looks—it's how it *tastes* that matters.

Did he dare to actually taste the next bite? Did he dare to let his tongue search out the grubs in the mayonnaise?

"Looks delicious, doesn't it?" Mr. Sudermann was saying to the crowd. "When *this* boy says he'll dig up a little something for lunch, he means it!"

Everyone laughed.

Andy picked up one of the fried worm bites. He thought of the delicious smell of the chicken in the Soul Food Kitchen and Carry-Out. Aunt Wanda's deep-fried batter smelled pretty good too. He put the worm in his mouth and swallowed without tasting. For a moment he thought it was stuck in his throat, just like in his dream —thought he might choke in front of the entire fifth-grade class. Then he felt it slide on down and reach his stomach at last. He took another bite and for just a moment let it linger. Was it possible . . . ? Yes, he was sure of it. Applesauce, just like the health inspector had said.

Jack was taking little nibbles of his sandwich from around the edge—grazing on the lettuce. He picked up a piece of fried worm and nibbled off a corner only, trying to usher it into his mouth by his teeth so that his lips wouldn't even touch it.

Well, he deserved it, Andy told himself, but all Jack had done, really, was giggle, and wouldn't Andy have done the same? He tried to think of the last really rotten thing Jack had done to him. Whatever it was, it had been a long time ago. Andy was good at holding grudges.

At that moment Sam reached out cautiously. "I'd like to try a bite of that sandwich, Andy," he said, and Andy knew he was only doing it to help.

"Why don't you eat Jack's?" he suggested, knowing that somehow, some way, he himself had to eat every bite of his own portion.

"*I* want to try something!" said Dora Kray's little brother who was too young to know better, and Jack shoved the fried worms toward him as though he couldn't give his food away fast enough.

"How about one more shot, now, of you two boys shaking hands?" the photographer said to Andy and Jack.

Jack was already standing, ready to run, and Andy stood up too and extended his hand, grinning at Jack.

Jack accepted it reluctantly.

"Pig face," he muttered as the camera clicked.

"Beetle breath," said Andy right back, but he smiled even more broadly.

Jack was smiling now in spite of himself.

"They're cousins," Mr. Sudermann was saying to the photographer. "Put that down in the photo caption." He smiled at the boys. "Maybe you fellas will grow up to be the next Wright brothers, who knows?"

Andy tried to imagine him and Jack inventing something together—actually spending time, dreaming up plans, seeing a project through. Somehow he imagined it very well.

"We might," he said, and walked back over to the pickup where Aunt Wanda stood waiting.